P9-DNL-182

Also by D. J. MacHale

Surrender the Key (The Library, Book 1)
Voyagers: Project Alpha
The SYLO Chronicles
Morpheus Road series
Pendragon series

THE LIBRARY

BOOK 2

BLACK MOON RISING

D. J. MacHale

Random House 🏠 New York

PH CASS COUNTY PUBLIC LIBRARY
400 E. MECHANIC
HARRISONVILLE, MO 64701

0 0022 0486522 0

To the terrific teachers and staff at
Manhattan Beach Middle School

This is a work of fiction. Names, characters, places, and incidents either
are the product of the author's imagination or are used fictitiously. Any resemblance to
actual persons, living or dead, events, or locales is entirely coincidental.

Text copyright © 2017 by D. J. MacHale
Jacket art copyright © 2017 by Vivienne To
Jacket concept copyright © 2017 by Vincent Chong
Key art copyright © 2017 by Bob Bianchini

All rights reserved. Published in the United States by Random House Children's Books,
a division of Penguin Random House LLC, New York.

Random House and the colophon are registered trademarks of
Penguin Random House LLC.

Visit us on the Web! randomhousekids.com

Educators and librarians, for a variety of teaching tools,
visit us at RHTeachersLibrarians.com

Library of Congress Cataloging-in-Publication Data:
Names: MacHale, D. J., author.
Title: Black Moon rising / D.J. MacHale.
Description: First edition. | New York : Random House, [2017] | Series: [The Library ;
book 2] | Summary: Middle-schoolers Marcus, Theo, and Lu return to the Library to help
figure out, and fix, what is going wrong at a school in Massachusetts.
Identifiers: LCCN 2016032224 | ISBN 978-1-101-93257-5 (hardcover) |
ISBN 978-1-101-93260-5 (trade pbk.) | ISBN 978-1-101-93258-2 (hardcover library binding) |
ISBN 978-1-101-93259-9 (ebook)
Subjects: | CYAC: Supernatural—Fiction. | Libraries—Fiction. | Middle schools—
Fiction. | Schools—Fiction. | Witchcraft—Fiction. | Mystery and detective stories.
Classification: LCC PZ7.M177535 Bkm 2017 | DDC [Fic]—dc23

Printed in the United States of America
10 9 8 7 6 5 4 3 2 1
First Edition

Random House Children's Books supports the First Amendment and
celebrates the right to read.

For a charm of powerful trouble,
Like a hell-broth boil and bubble.
Double, double toil and trouble;
Fire burn, and cauldron bubble.

—FROM *Macbeth,* BY WILLIAM SHAKESPEARE

FOREWORD

So, you've decided to come back, aye?

Brave of you. I like that. Not just because you enjoy my books, but because you have a decidedly weird streak. That's a compliment. You're my kind of people. Though I'm not able to fully explain why I like to write stories about the strange and supernatural, I also don't understand why I enjoy reading them so much.

I'll bet *you* can't explain why you like reading them either.

What is it about spooky stories that attracts us? Do we like it when our hearts race as the characters we care about grow closer to danger? Is it fun to imagine exactly what form of dastardly evil lurks in every dark shadow, ready to spring? Is it about the challenge of trying to fit together the puzzle pieces of a dangerous mystery? Or maybe it's about the relief we feel when, no matter how horrific an experience our characters might go through, we always know we can close the book and make it all go away?

Unless, that is, the shadows choose to stick around and haunt our dreams.

The answers, I think, are yes, yes, yes, and yes. All of the above. We have vivid imaginations. I've been writing spooky stories for a very long time now, and one thing I've learned is that the people who enjoy them most are the ones who can put their logical minds on a shelf (assuming they have a logical mind . . . and a shelf) and open up their thoughts to possibility.

That's what you'll find plenty of in the Library. Possibility. As Everett the librarian says in *Surrender the Key,* "There are forces at work in this world that we know little about. Situations come up all the time that defy the normal rules of science and nature. Strange things. Oddities. Unexplainable phenomena."

You may or may not believe that to be the case in real life, but when you step into the Library, you know you've entered a world where it's the absolute truth.

That's why you've come back.

As always, I'd like to acknowledge some of the many people who have helped bring this latest tome to you.

We authors have a great relationship with readers. What we write, you read. There's a direct line. But that line is populated with hundreds of people without whom you and I wouldn't be able to have this relationship.

Most of these good folks are with Random House Children's Books. It all starts with the editorial team of Diane Landolf, Michelle Nagler, and Mallory Loehr. Beyond that talented trio are art directors and artists and salespeople and marketers and publicists and the many people who support them. From there we have distributors and booksellers, librarians and teachers, book fairs and book festivals. All play a role in taking my words and getting them to you.

At my end are Richard Curtis and Peter Nelson, my terrific agent and lawyer. I have a wonderful family who allow me to have a job that is kind of eerie and supernatural in and of itself. I've got a dog that keeps me company by sitting at my feet as I write and only wants an occasional walk and treat in return.

I've just skimmed the surface here, but rest assured that each of these individuals has played an important role in the creation of this book. So if you have nightmares tonight, throw a little blame their way too, would ya?

Okay, our time together grows short. The Paradox key is warming up.

The Library beckons.

Who knows what you'll find once you step through the door?

Well, I do. And soon . . . you will too.

Slip the key into the lock, turn, feel the bolt release with a solid *click*. Now open the door.

We're back.

Have fun and . . . pleasant dreams.

D. J. MacHale, 2017

Prologue

Middle school isn't supposed to be dangerous.

Not normally, anyway.

But there was nothing normal about the string of horrible events that were unfolding at Coppell Middle School. The fall semester had begun like any other but quickly turned into one that nobody would ever forget.

Though most would like to.

Some thought the school was jinxed. Others felt it was nothing more than a run of incredibly bad luck. None could deny that a nefarious black cloud had drifted over the school, one that was producing impossible waves of serious misfortune.

No one knew why it was happening, when it would end . . .

1

. . . or *if* it would end.

It was the first basketball pep rally of the season. The bleachers in the gym were packed with hundreds of amped-up kids who were there to cheer for their team. The school band occupied one end of the bleachers, gamely pushing through a weak version of "Uptown Funk." The booming rhythm pounded out by the drum line completely drowned out the brass section and gave no hope to the woodwinds. Nobody complained. It wasn't a very good band anyway.

Teachers sat on the bottom row. Normally they'd be scattered throughout the crowd to make sure the kids kept quiet, but since the entire purpose of a pep rally was to make noise, they sat on their hands and let the energy flow.

The pep squad was on the opposite end of the bleachers from the band, shouting out cheers that had nothing to do with what the band was playing. Cheerleaders did cartwheels and flips across the gym floor. The kids screamed every time one of them stuck a landing. They screamed even louder when the cheerleaders missed and landed on their butts. They screamed when the pep squad waved their streamers and when the bandleader swung his baton.

Basically they just screamed.

It was semiorganized chaos, and the basketball team hadn't even shown up yet.

Presiding over the mayhem was the eighth-grade class

president, Ainsley Murcer. She was stationed on the opposite side of the gym, across from the bleachers, along with the AV teacher, who was running the soundboard. Ainsley had planned every detail of the extravaganza. She'd choreographed the entire show, down to the split second, for maximum dramatic effect. She wanted the band to play one tune, then hand the show off to the pep squad for some cheers. The pep squad would then give way to the cheerleaders, who would wow everyone with their daring acrobatics before stepping aside for the principal to make a speech. The buildup to the dramatic climax would come when the band played the school fight song, which would herald the grand entrance of the basketball team.

It was all set in Ainsley's mind. It would be perfect.

Except it was more like perfect bedlam because everything happened at once.

"The band shouldn't be playing now," Ainsley complained to the AV teacher. "Nobody can hear the pep squad, and the cheerleaders are just randomly showing off."

The teacher gave her a sympathetic look and shrugged. The train was on the tracks and picking up speed. It was out of their hands.

"When do I talk?" Mr. Jackson, the school principal, shouted to Ainsley.

"Soon," Ainsley said, trying to sound as if everything were under control. She had sold the principal on a pep

3

rally, but it was quickly rolling toward anarchy. She shoved a microphone into his hands and said, "I'll cue you."

"You want me to quiet them down?" Mr. Jackson asked.

"No!" Ainsley said forcefully. "I've got this. I'll get the band to stop so the pep squad can do their cheer."

Ainsley was determined to wrest back control. As she ran toward the bleachers, she passed a group of boys who stood along one wall, looking bored. They seemed far too cool to be hanging out at a pep rally.

"How's it goin', Murcer?" one of the guys called to Ainsley. It was Nate Christmas, the ringleader. He loved the fact that Ainsley's perfect plan was going sideways.

"Great!" Ainsley called to him cheerfully as she ran past. "Couldn't be better."

Nate shared a laugh with his friends and then motioned for them to head out.

As Ainsley approached the band, she caught sight of a girl sitting halfway up the bleachers. She was crushed against the wall by a crowd of frenzied kids who didn't even realize she was there. She stood out because she was the only kid not yelling and cheering or having so much as an ounce of fun. Her name was Kayla Eggers, and from the pained look on her face, it was clear she wanted to be as far away from this madness as possible.

Ainsley made eye contact with Kayla and gave a small shrug as if to say, *Sorry.*

Kayla didn't react. She just shrank even further.

Ainsley ran up to the band director. "Stop the song!" she shouted.

"What did you say?" the director shouted back.

"Stop! You aren't supposed to play yet!"

"Thank you!" the director yelled. "We'll play another if you want!"

"NO! Just finish!"

Ainsley spun to head back to the soundboard and collided with a cheerleader in mid-roundoff. The two fell to the floor in a tangle of arms and legs as laughter rained down on them from the bleachers.

"What are you doing?" the cheerleader shouted angrily. "Go away!"

"Sorry, sorry," Ainsley said, and helped her to her feet.

The cheerleader pulled away in a huff, plastered on a smile, and did another tumbling run.

Ainsley ran back to the soundboard, where Mr. Jackson was waiting patiently.

"Let me get this under control!" he called to her above the noise.

"No, this is my show!" Ainsley barked at him.

Mr. Jackson stiffened. He wasn't used to being spoken to like that by a student.

"Sorry," Ainsley said, trying to recover. "I'm just a little . . . stressed."

"Yeah, I get that," Mr. Jackson replied.

A huge cheer went up. Now what?

The basketball team had arrived. The players trotted out in single file between the two sets of bleachers and jogged to center court. The crowd noise blew through the roof. The bandleader finally stopped the song. Just as well, since nobody was listening anyway.

The players circled up at center court, dribbling basketballs and passing them to each other. The booming sound of the bouncing balls and the added excitement shot the decibel level back up to earsplitting.

"When do I talk?" Mr. Jackson shouted to Ainsley.

"You were supposed to talk before the players came out," Ainsley snapped with frustration. "Why is this happening? This is horrible!"

"At least it can't get any worse," the AV teacher said.

He was wrong.

Crack. Crack. Crack.

The sound of multiple sharp explosions tore through the gym. Kids gasped and cried out in surprise. Somebody had lit a string of firecrackers beneath the bleachers ... directly below where Kayla Eggers was sitting.

As the loud, snapping *pops* continued, Kayla pressed herself even harder against the wall while the kids around her pushed away from the spot, shoving each other to escape from ground zero. The rapid-fire explosions may have lasted only a few seconds, but the terrifying damage was done. The crowd noise died. The cheering ended. The basketballs stopped bouncing.

Kayla sat alone, directly above the spot where the mayhem occurred. Smoke floated up from beneath her seat as she cowered next to the cinder-block wall, paralyzed with fear and quietly crying.

Hundreds of people silently looked her way, momentarily stunned.

While everyone else was focused on Kayla, Ainsley's eye was caught by movement elsewhere.

Coming out from beneath the bleachers was Nate Christmas.

That was it. Ainsley's rage and frustration boiled over. She grabbed the microphone from Mr. Jackson and punched the On switch. After a quick screech of ear-piercing feedback, she had the floor.

"I see you, Nate Christmas!"

Her angry voice boomed through the overhead speakers and echoed across the otherwise silent gym.

Everyone's attention snapped to Ainsley.

That's when it happened.

The section of bleachers where Kayla was sitting began to tremble. It was as if an earthquake had hit the gym, but the only people who felt it were those still on the bleachers. The kids panicked and pushed their way forward to get off the structure.

Kayla was too confused and petrified to move.

The kids tumbled over one another, desperate to escape.

"Kayla!" Ainsley shouted.

There was a gut-wrenching sound of twisting steel as a section of bleachers pulled away from the wall and collapsed like a monstrous accordion. Most every kid screamed in horror as the heavy structure twisted and crumpled, forcing many to dive the rest of the way to safety. Within seconds the entire section had fallen into a heap of bent metal and splintered wood.

There was a long, frozen moment when everyone stared at the destruction in disbelief. Mr. Jackson and a few teachers were the first to break the spell and react. While the kids backed away, the adults ran straight toward the ruined structure to pull students to safety.

Miraculously, no one had been seriously injured. There were plenty of bruises and scrapes and one broken foot, but nothing life-threatening.

Once the dust settled, there was only one student left on the pile of wood and steel that had once been bleachers. Kayla lay in the center of the rubble with her head buried in her arms, sobbing.

Ainsley stood alone in the center of the gym, staring at

the devastation and at the little lost girl who couldn't bring herself to move.

A young teacher, Mr. Martin, climbed over the wreckage, scooped Kayla up in his arms, and carried her away from danger.

"You okay?" he asked.

Kayla sniffed and nodded.

He gently set her on her feet, and another young teacher, Ms. Tomac, put an arm around the girl and guided her away while gently wiping away her tears.

Kayla wasn't the only one sobbing. Now that the shock had worn off, many of the kids huddled together on the far side of the gym were in tears. For some, they were tears of relief. Others were overcome with emotion, realizing how close they had come to disaster. Most were left stunned by the sudden, violent nature of the event.

It wasn't the first strange and dangerous accident that had happened at Coppell Middle School that fall. It was simply the next.

The whispers had begun. And the rumors. Whatever was happening wasn't natural. Something was seriously wrong.

Middle school isn't supposed to be dangerous.

CHAPTER

1

"I'm dead. I'm dead. I'm seriously dead."

"You're also a drama queen," Theo McLean said without a trace of sympathy. "It's not exactly the end of the world."

"Easy for you to say," Lu snapped at him. "What did you get on the test? An A, right?"

"No, in fact, I didn't," Theo replied. "I got an A-*plus*. But I missed the extra credit."

"I hate you," Lu snarled.

My two best buddies don't always get along. If not for me, I doubt they'd even be friends. Annabella Lu is driven by emotion. She's a real "seat of the pants" kind of girl who always starts out in third gear. Theo McLean, on the other hand, is a thinker. An overthinker, actually.

By the time he analyzes a problem and looks at every possible solution from multiple angles, it's usually the next day and nobody can remember what the problem was in the first place.

I fall somewhere in the middle. I can think through a challenge fast, and I'm not afraid to make bold, decisive choices. On the other hand, my bold decisions aren't always the best, and I've been known to solve problems by creating even bigger problems. But, hey, at least I get things done. Sort of.

Lu is Asian American, Theo is African American, and I'm Caucasian Euro-mutt-American. Together we look like the cast of some racially diverse kids' TV show.

"It's only one test grade," I said, trying to be the voice of reason. "Your father's not going to kill you over one C."

"It's not just one C, Marcus," Lu said, spinning on her roller skates with nervous energy.

Lu is a roller-derby girl. The only reason she takes off her skates during the day is because they aren't allowed on Stony Brook Middle School property. Theo and I were sitting near the school's front entrance so Lu could legally roll along the sidewalk and burn off tension.

"I bombed a couple of other science tests I haven't told my parents about, and now I'm staring at a big, fat

11

old C for the trimester. That will make my dad's brain detonate."

"It won't. Your parents are cool," I argued.

"Sure, when it comes to my friends and letting me play derby and not getting up in my stuff all the time, but school is a whole different thing. I've got a tiger mom and a dragon dad. To them, anything less than an A is failing."

"So what will they do?" Theo asked.

"I don't know!" Lu shouted in frustration. "I've never had to find out! They could ground me, or get me a tutor, or they might even force me to quit derby!"

"All because of one lousy C?" I asked, incredulous.

"To them it's not a lousy C. It's a hot blade that cuts straight into their souls and twists with such a vengeance that pain from the hideous scar will torture them until the day they die."

"Wow," I said. "You may suck at science but I bet you're getting an A in English."

"So do better next time," Theo said matter-of-factly. "I mean, you're not dumb. Not really."

"Gee, thanks," Lu said, her voice dripping with sarcasm. "Maybe that should go on my tombstone: 'Here lies Annabella Lu. She wasn't dumb. Not really.'"

"But you aren't," Theo said innocently.

"Ugh," Lu groaned, and skated off. She spun around,

skating backward, and said, "If you don't see me tomorrow, it's because I've been shipped off to boarding school."

"You're making too big a thing outta this!" I called to her as she spun back around and zipped away.

Her response was to throw me a dismissive wave.

"I don't know why her parents would be so upset," Theo said. "I mean, maybe a C is the best she can do."

I stood and hoisted my pack. "I'd keep that opinion to myself, unless you want roller-skate tracks across your back."

Theo stood too and said, "So what did *you* get on the test?"

"An A-plus," I replied without hesitation. "Nailed the extra credit too. Do *not* tell Lu."

Theo and I live close to the school and always walk home together through our suburban neighborhood in Stony Brook, Connecticut. It was late October, and the fall foliage was at its spectacular peak. The leafy trees sported stunning shades of orange, yellow, and red that made the sky seem freakishly blue. It was like something out of a perfect Halloween picture book.

As we walked along, Theo kept glancing at me as if he wanted to say something but couldn't find the guts. The whole time he was tugging on his earlobe. It's a nervous tic that always shows up when he's thinking hard.

"What!" I finally exclaimed, making him jump.

"It's nothing," he said quickly, which meant it was definitely something. "Forget it."

"Okay," I said with a dismissive shrug.

He pulled on his earlobe again and said, "But it actually is something."

"Aha!"

"C'mon, Marcus, we have to talk about it."

"About what?" I asked, though I knew exactly what he meant.

"It's been over a week, and we haven't discussed it once. It's like we're pretending it didn't happen."

"I'm not sure what you mean," I said innocently.

"Give me a break," he said with impatience.

"Oh! You mean about how the three of us trapped a centuries-old evil spirit in a metal box and tossed it into the Long Island Sound so it could never escape and terrorize people ever again? Is that what you're talking about?"

"Yes, smart guy. That. And the Library."

The Library.

Theo was right. I was trying to pretend like none of it had happened. I hadn't been back since we captured the Boggin.

"I know," I said sincerely. "I've been avoiding."

"I thought you wanted to help Everett finish some of the stories. What's the problem?"

"No problem," I said. "It's just that the whole thing seems like a dream. I mean, you saw those shelves. There were thousands of unfinished stories there. How can I hope to put a dent in that?"

"Maybe not a dent, but you could finish a few. Like maybe . . . oh, I don't know . . . *mine*. Or Lu's."

He had me there. The unfinished stories in the Library were about people who had experienced unexplainable events. Odd occurrences. Supernatural shenanigans. The only thing the stories had in common was that they were unfinished. Throughout history the agents of the Library were able to step into those stories—don't ask me how—and work to try and solve them.

Like my biological father before me, I was an agent of the Library. Lucky me. I didn't ask for the job, but it was mine anyway.

Making things even more complicated, both Theo and Lu feared they were going through their own weirdness. Lu's cousin had mysteriously vanished without a trace. Nobody in her family had any idea of what might have happened to her. Theo's deal was that he had had his fortune told by one of those goofy arcade machines at an amusement park. It was an ominous prediction that life as he knew it would end on his fourteenth birthday. Not a big deal except that both of his brothers had their fortunes told at the same time and both came true.

Theo and Lu feared, or maybe hoped, that their stories could be found somewhere on the shelves of the Library along with all the other unfinished stories. If so, there was a chance we could solve the mysteries. I'd promised them I would look into it, but I was having trouble getting up the nerve to go back.

"We got lucky with the Boggin," I said. "Things could just as easily have gone south."

"What about your father's story?" Theo asked. "Your biological father. And mother. I thought you wanted to find the truth about how they died?"

"I do but—"

"But what?" he exclaimed, exasperated. "I can't explain how that library exists and how spirits are able to write stories about—what did Everett call them, disruptions? Or how the agents can finish those stories. But it's real and there's a ton at stake."

"I know, I get it!" I said, annoyed. "But it's a lot to wrap my head around, you know? I'm just a little bit . . ."

I couldn't finish the sentence.

Theo finished it for me.

"Scared?"

"Yeah. Scared. Okay? Do you blame me?"

"Not for a second," Theo said. "I don't want you to do anything you're uncomfortable with. It was just a dumb fortune-telling machine. I'm sure I'll live through my birthday."

I stopped walking and looked him square in the eye. "Now you're laying guilt on me?"

"Sorry. I'm really not. But just so you know, if you ever want to go back, I'm with you. And Lu is annoying, but she'll go too. Remember that, okay?"

"Yeah, sure."

We got to my street and split up to go to our own houses. When I got home, I went right to my room and tried to do homework. *Tried.* How could I focus on algebra when all I could think about was the heavy, old-fashioned brass key that hung around my neck? There were many times over the past week that I was tempted to put the key near a door to create the magic that allowed me to enter the Library. I was torn between wanting to jump into a new adventure and fearing where the stories I found might lead.

This wasn't fantasy. It was all very real. We dodged a bullet when we captured the Boggin. Others weren't so lucky. People died. Part of me wanted to quit while I was ahead, and pretend the Library was just some strange dream I could wake up from and forget about. I might have done exactly that if my best friends weren't possibly going through their own disruptions.

And the Library gave me a chance to solve the mystery of how my birth parents died. Not knowing them or who I really was had haunted me my whole life. Getting the Paradox key was like a gift from the grave. From the past. From *my* past. My biological father wanted me to have it. He wanted me to know the truth about him and my mother, and their deaths. How could I not follow through? And how could I not try to help my friends?

With all that at stake, how could I possibly pretend the Library didn't exist?

I don't think I slept much that night. I held on to the Paradox key, running my fingers over the details of its elaborate carvings and trying to get past the feeling of dread. By the time morning came, I hadn't gotten any closer to making a decision about what to do.

Maybe I wasn't so good at making bold, decisive choices after all.

"Marcus! Breakfast!"

Mom and Dad were already sitting at the kitchen table. I immediately sensed tension. I was good at that. I'd had a lot of practice. They were always on me about something and that morning was no different.

"Family discussion time," Mom announced as I sat down.

Uh-oh. I knew what that meant. I was about to be hit with something I wouldn't like.

"What's up?" I asked innocently.

"Mom and I have been talking," Dad began.

Uh-oh again. That was never good news. I hated it when they talked. Especially when it was about me. It was never a discussion that led to them giving me an award or something. No, whatever was headed my way, it would be bad.

"You're doing well in school," Dad said. "We're proud of you."

I wanted to jump up and say, "Thanks! Good talk. Have a nice day!" and get out of there. But I knew that wouldn't fly.

"But life isn't just about school," he said.

I couldn't argue with that.

"What I mean is, we want you to branch out a little and get involved with some after-school activities. You know, extracurricular things."

"Like what?" I asked skeptically.

"Like anything," Mom said. "Play a sport. Join a club. Volunteer somewhere. Maybe take music lessons. There's a whole lot of time between school and dinner when you could be doing something constructive. There's more to getting an education than homework."

I couldn't argue with that either.

"Besides," Dad said, "and don't take this the wrong

way, but let's be honest: you don't really study all that hard and you still get straight A's."

Again, no argument. School was cake.

"That's awesome," Dad added. "We're proud of you, but we'd like to see you challenge yourself a little."

"Okay, I'll think about it," I said, and dug into my cereal, hoping my answer would satisfy them.

No such luck. I could sense the two of them exchanging looks, silently debating about who would fire the next shot.

"We're serious, Marcus," Mom said. "It's important that you experience as much as you can. It'll also help you make new friends."

"What's wrong with my *old* friends?" I asked.

"Nothing," Mom said quickly. "But you've been hanging around with the same two kids pretty much your whole life. Maybe you should broaden your horizons a little."

"Look," I said curtly. "I like my horizons where they are. I'm not going to join the chess club. Or the yearbook. Or the paper-freaking-airplane club. That's not me. Maybe I'll run track, but that's not until the spring. I think I'm doing pretty well. I get good grades and I don't get into trouble."

That prompted another look between the two of them.

"Okay," I added. "I don't get into *much* trouble, so let's just leave well enough alone, okay?"

"Don't get angry," Dad said. "We're just thinking about what's best for you."

"I don't need help. I'm doing fine. I don't need to join some group of geek—"

My words caught in my throat as I felt a strange sensation. At first I thought I might be getting sick. Or having some kind of attack. It took me a second to understand what it really was.

The Paradox key was growing warm against my chest.

"What's the matter?" Dad asked.

I opened my mouth to answer, but no words came out. Mostly because I didn't have any. At least none I wanted to give. Mom and Dad had no idea about the Library, and I wasn't going to tell them either.

The key was growing warmer. For a second I feared it might burn a hole in my shirt. Or my chest.

"I . . . I . . . I gotta go to the bathroom," I said, and ran for the stairs.

As I sprinted out of the room, Dad said to Mom, "Did the milk go sour?"

I took the stairs two at a time, went straight for the bathroom, and closed the door. I reached for the cord around my neck that held the ancient brass key and

21

pulled it over my head. The key was definitely warm. I clutched it in my hand and felt it pulse with life, or whatever it was that magical keys pulsed with.

It had never done this before. It was almost like it was calling to me. Was that possible?

There was only one way to find out.

What had started to feel like a dream was about to become reality once again.

I reached the key toward the closed bathroom door and felt its warmth spread through my hand and up my arm. As I moved it closer to the door, a familiar dark spot appeared beneath the doorknob. The dark spot grew and transformed into a round brass plate with an old-fashioned keyhole. I slipped the key inside until it fit snugly into the tumblers.

It was as though the key had made the decision I couldn't make for myself.

"My parents want me to broaden my horizons?" I said. "I'd say this is about as extracurricular as it gets."

I twisted the key and heard the solid *click* of the lock releasing. With my other hand I grasped the doorknob, turned, and pulled.

The door opened easily . . .

. . . and I stepped into the Library.

CHAPTER
2

"Everett!" I called out to the old-guy spirit who was the curator of the strange library.

My call echoed back from the dark recesses of the ancient room. Nothing had changed since I'd been there the last time, which was no surprise. The place looked as though it had been around since the 1800s, so why would I expect anything to be different after a week?

Several gas lamps hung from the walls and gave off a warm, flickering light. Everett said that time had no meaning in the Library. I guess that's why there were no windows. Seeing the sun move across the sky would definitely mean time was passing. But that made me wonder: What exactly *was* outside? Where was this library? Outer space? Limbo? The Twilight Zone?

To my left were multiple aisles of polished wood shelves filled with thousands of unfinished books . . . the reason the Library existed. To my right were the aisles of books that had been finished by the agents of the Library. There wasn't a speck of dust anywhere. Did that mean Everett walked around with a dust rag and a mop? Or was that the job of other spirits? Or if time truly didn't mean anything here, maybe dust didn't have the chance to settle. I had no idea.

I walked quickly to the circulation desk, expecting to see Everett perched on his stool reading.

He wasn't.

Maybe he was off dusting somewhere.

I was suddenly feeling very alone.

"Everett!" I called out again, louder.

"Easy!" he bellowed from directly behind me, making me jump. "You'll wake the dead." He chuckled and added, "Then again, I'm already up."

Everett looked to be in his seventies. He was short and balding with a horseshoe of white hair that looped around the back of his head. His cheeks were covered with bushy muttonchop sideburns, and he wore wire-rimmed glasses so delicate that the lenses looked as though they were floating in front of his eyes. He had on gray tweedy pants, with a matching vest over a pure-white shirt that had the sleeves rolled up. Like the Library, he looked like he was straight out of the 1800s.

And, oh yeah, he was a ghost.

"What's with the key?" I asked. "It got hot. Is that some kind of Bat-Signal to get me to come here?"

"You could say that," Everett said with his slight Irish accent. "I had to do something to get your attention."

He waddled to the end of one of the aisles where a wooden podium stood. It was the podium that always held the next book that needed to be finished.

There was a small red volume resting on top.

"Yeah, well, I've been . . . busy," I said, staring at the unopened book.

"Busy? Or maybe you've just been scared," he said with a wry wink.

"I wasn't! I was just . . . just . . . Okay, I was scared. So what?"

"No shame in that, lad. This is still new to you. But something came up that needs our attention, so I thought it wise to give you a wee bit of a nudge."

"Is it about Lu's missing cousin?" I asked, hopefully.

"No."

"Theo's fortune?"

"No."

I deflated.

"Did you even look?"

Everett frowned. "Take a look around, boy-o. Do you have any idea how many volumes I have to wade through?"

"No."

"Neither do I. But there are plenty! I've been searching for your friends' stories, I promise you. But I'm a spirit, not magical. It'll take some time."

"And time means nothing here, right?"

"Right you are, but I did come across something that appears to have some time sensitivity. That does happen every so often."

He put his hand on the red book and patted it a few times.

"A new story?" I asked.

"Not just new. It's now. This isn't about something that happened in the past. The events chronicled in this book are happening right now. Today, in your time. That's why it can't wait."

It was crazy how spirits were everywhere, observing strange events and documenting them to create these books. It made me incredibly self-conscious about going to the bathroom.

"Give me the highlights," I said.

Everett picked up the book and flipped through the pages.

"It concerns a school in Massachusetts. Coppell Middle School. It's an understatement to say the folks there have been going through a spell of bad luck, but that's about the size of it. Here, read a wee bit."

He handed the open book to me and pointed to a paragraph that read:

Since the school year began, a series of accidents have occurred that go beyond what could be considered normal. It started out innocently enough. A cart full of glassware went tumbling, though no one was anywhere near it; windows cracked and shattered for no apparent reason; a grease fire broke out in the cafeteria kitchen. At first none of the incidents were serious. Nobody was hurt. But the accidents grew worse. An electrical transformer blew up, knocking out the school's power; a climbing rope in the gym snapped while a boy was halfway up; and a groundskeeper lost control of a riding lawn mower that leveled an entire rose garden.

"Glad I don't go to *that* school," I said.

"Aye, and it gets even worse. A young lady driving by the school suddenly swerved and drove her vehicle onto the property, through a glass door, and straight into the dining hall during lunchtime. She was completely rattled, as you might imagine. Said it was like the car had a mind of its own."

"Dining hall?"

"Cafeteria. Whatever it is you call it. Spare me your criticism."

Everett grabbed the book back and waddled down the aisle, headed for the long circulation desk.

I followed right behind him.

"That's some seriously bad luck."

"Aye. And now it's risen to a whole different level. They were having a sports gathering in their gymnasium. A pep rally, I believe it's called. With no warning or apparent reason, a whole section of bleachers collapsed."

"Oh man. Did anybody get hurt?"

"No one too badly, thank goodness. There's a pattern here. The severity of the events is escalating. Quickly. What's happening at that school goes beyond the logic that governs normal events. In my mind, that elevates it into something else entirely."

"A disruption," I said.

"Aye. Something is happening there, Marcus. Something wrong. I fear it's only a matter of time before someone is seriously hurt, or worse."

"What do you think's causing it?" I asked.

Everett dropped the book onto the circulation desk and said, "That's where you come in."

"Me? How? I can't just go to Massachusetts."

"Ah, but you can."

He opened the book to show me a cream-colored card with dark lines that was glued inside the cover. It was the kind of card they used to use in library books to show the due date. Before computers, that is.

"All you have to do is check out the book."

"Then what?"

"Then the book is yours for a while," he said, as if it were the most obvious thing in the world. "When you leave here, you'll be a part of the story."

"So I walk back out the door and I'm suddenly in Massachusetts and at that school?"

"Not exactly. If you walk out the door you came in through, you'd be back home. The door that gets you into the story is on the far side of the Library."

It all sounded so mystically ridiculous, except I knew it wasn't.

"Why didn't I have to do that with the Boggin story?" I asked.

"Because you were already part of that story. This is different. You have no connection to the events happening in Massachusetts."

My head was spinning.

"Okay, so I go to the school. Then what? I'm no detective."

"That's what your father said at first too, but he always found a way. Finished many of these stories, he did. Seeing how you handled the Boggin, I suspect you'll do every bit as well."

My heart raced. As much as I knew this was what the Library was all about, I wasn't so sure I was ready to play along.

"I don't know—"

"Look, lad," Everett said. "You've finished one story already. Because of you and your friends, Michael Swenor's spirit was put to rest and you stopped the Boggin from spreading more misery. You know how important our work is. Your father knew it too."

"And he died for it," I said softly.

"Possibly," Everett said. "We don't know that for a fact. But if there's any hope of finding out exactly why he and your mother died, you'll need to embrace the Library and how it works. Not just for the people you'll be helping but for yourself as well."

Ever since I discovered the Library, I knew that at some point I'd have to step up to the plate, enter one of the unfinished stories, and try to fill my father's shoes. Now that it was really happening, I was having second thoughts. And third thoughts.

"My parents think I'm in the bathroom," I said lamely.

Everett chuckled. "And when you step back into your house, it'll be as if you never left."

"But what if I'm in Massachusetts for a long time? Won't I get tired? And hungry? I can't just spend a whole bunch of time somewhere else and then pick up where I left off at home."

"So take a nap and eat something!" Everett said with a touch of impatience.

I had this weird fear that I was about to pull a Rip Van Winkle and come back as an old man.

"You can step out of the story anytime you'd like," Everett said, as if reading my thoughts. "The Paradox key will get you right back here."

Everett reached under the counter and brought out an old-fashioned fountain pen. He held it out to me.

"What's that for?" I asked.

"Sign the card," Everett said, "and the book be yours."

I looked at the pen, then at the book that contained an unfinished story about a middle school that was . . . what? Haunted? Cursed? Incredibly unlucky? Whatever the truth was, it was up to me to find it. Like my father before me, I was an agent of the Library.

I took the pen.

"Sign on the top line," Everett instructed.

I leaned down, staring at the blank card. Nobody had checked this book out before. I was the first. This was crazy.

But I signed.

When I handed the pen back to Everett, he was smiling broadly.

"I remember the first time your father did that," he said. "He looked about as nervous as you do right now."

"That's not comforting."

"You'll be fine. I know you will."

"So what happens now? Do I take the book with me?"

Everett blew on my signature to dry it, then gently closed the cover.

"If you'd like, but I suggest you leave it here. We don't want it getting lost like that other book."

I knew exactly what he meant. The last book my father had been working on was a story about the Boggin. It never made its way back to the Library and my father and mother died. Somehow, some way, I had to find that book and finish their story. But not just then.

"So where's the door out of here?" I asked.

"You mean the door into the story."

"Whatever! Where do I go?"

Everett tucked the book under his arm and led me past more aisles of books and deeper into the Library. For a second I feared I'd get lost in the ancient labyrinth, but that was the least of my worries. We reached what turned out to be the final aisle, rounded the corner, and stood facing another wooden door that looked pretty much the same as the one I'd come through from home.

"So I go through and I'll be at that school?"

"Aye."

"And I can come back anytime?"

"Just use the Paradox key."

I touched the key and pressed it against my chest. No way was I ever going to let go of that thing.

"No guarantees," I said.

"There are never guarantees," Everett said. "Especially when dealing with stories from the Library."

I walked slowly toward the wooden door, feeling like I was walking the last few yards to the gallows. I stepped right up to it, reached for the doorknob, and stopped.

"What do I do first?" I asked.

"Up to you. But remember this: disruptions happen for a reason. When things go awry, it's because someone caused it. Or some*thing*."

"Like the Boggin."

"Aye. It always comes down to people, Marcus. Living or dead. Somebody at that school knows why the disruption is happening. It could be intentional, or they may have no idea they're involved. Ask questions. Be observant. The clues will be there."

I nodded. Not because I knew what to do, but because I understood the full weight of my task, I grabbed the doorknob and twisted until the latch released and the door opened a crack.

"This won't hurt, will it?"

"Not a bit," Everett said. "It's just like stepping through a normal door . . . and into another life."

"Normal? Yeah, right."

If I had taken another second to think about what those words truly meant, I would have slammed that door, run the other way, and gone home. But I was committed. I didn't know if I had any hope of solving the mystery of the cursed school, but I had to give it a shot.

It's what I was meant to do.

Before I could change my mind, I yanked the door open and, as the old spirit had said . . .

. . . stepped into another life.

CHAPTER

3

Actually, I stepped through the door and into a bathroom.

At first I thought I was back home, that the magic of the Library hadn't worked. But I stood facing a line of urinals that were definitely not in my bathroom at home.

Neither were the three guys who stood in front of the sinks, jamming paper into the drains to clog them up so the sinks would overflow. They were laughing like it was the most ingenious prank ever devised. The only problem was that they couldn't figure out how to keep the water running—it kept shutting off after a couple of seconds.

These were not rocket scientists.

"Leave one of your books on the lever to keep it down," one of the geniuses said to another.

"I'm not leaving my book!" was the reply.

"Why not? It's not like you read it!"

The third guy laughed.

Yeah. Morons.

I'd stepped out of a closet. If I reopened the door, I'd probably find a mop and a bunch of rolls of toilet paper. To get back to the Library, I'd have to use the Paradox key.

I didn't get the chance to test that theory, because as soon as the door closed behind me with a loud *thunk,* the three stooges whipped around in surprise to see me standing there. There was a frozen moment of confusion, as if they couldn't understand how I had shown up so suddenly.

"Where did you come from?" one guy said accusingly, like I had tried to sneak up on them. He must have been the alpha dog, because the others kept their eyes on him as he took a step toward me. He was short and wore a saggy hoodie over a black T-shirt that simply said WICKED. I knew guys like this from my own school. They traveled in packs and tried to look dangerous.

"Where do you think I came from?" I replied.

The short guy stopped suddenly. The look of surprise on his face almost made me laugh. I don't think he was used to having a question answered with a question.

"He saw what we were doing, Nate," one of his pals

said nervously, like I'd caught them pulling off the crime of the century.

"Nate," I said quickly, "this is where you guys hang out? A bathroom?"

Nate, the leader, was totally off balance, which was exactly what I was going for.

"Who the hell are you?" he asked.

"Tell you what, chief," I said. "I'll do you a favor and forget what I saw here."

I took a step toward the exit, but Nate's hand shot out and grabbed my shirt. This was the critical moment. I never back down from a fight, especially not with a guy a lot smaller than me. And I don't like bullies. Normally, I'd welcome the chance to hammer this guy. I've been known to get in a fight or two. Or three. But his two friends made it tricky. Besides, a fight would end my investigation before it even began.

"How about if I do you a favor and kick your butt?" he said, staring me square in the eye.

I laughed. I couldn't help it. The guy was trying to be threatening and clever, but he was neither.

My laugh threw him. Clowns like this were used to their victims cowering in fear.

"I'll do you an even bigger favor," I said. "You want that faucet to run? Stick a penny behind the lever. That'll keep it from shutting off."

I stuck my hand into my pocket, pulled out a penny, and flipped it to him.

Nate let go of my shirt and caught the coin.

I took the opportunity to back away. These idiots had no idea what to do. They just stared at me, dumbfounded, as I strolled casually to the exit and got out of there.

I had no idea if the penny thing would actually work. I hoped it wouldn't, or I'd be partially responsible for flooding the school. But I couldn't worry about that, and I walked away quickly, hoping to blend into the crowd of kids before Nate and his merry men came after me. Or water started flowing out from under the bathroom door.

Once I was clear, I slowed down and got my first look at Coppell Middle School. Right off the bat I saw that it was nothing like Stony Brook Middle School. My school was modern, with wide corridors, brightly colored walls, and lots of windows that let in sunlight. This place was dark and full of shadows. The walls were made of brown brick, and the only natural light came in through narrow windows near the ceiling. Curved archways led from corridor to corridor, and the floors weren't covered with tile or linoleum but real wood. The smell was different too. Stony Brook always smelled like disinfectant. This place smelled like . . .

mold. It seemed more like Hogwarts than a modern middle school.

On the other hand, it was also totally familiar. The halls were packed. Some kids hurried through, while others just hung out. Turned out that kids from Massachusetts looked pretty much the same as kids from Connecticut. Or probably from anywhere else.

Massachusetts.

I was in Massa-freaking-chusetts. I had stepped out of the Library and been transported to another state. Another state of mind too. It's tough enough figuring out where you belong in your own school. I was now in alien territory with no friends to rely on. I didn't belong there. At some point a teacher was bound to corner me.

I pulled out my phone to check the time, but the clock wasn't working. I couldn't get a cell signal either; all it did was show me a home screen. Basically, it was useless. I guess when you drop into a story courtesy of the Library, you can't make calls home. Or play *Temple Run*.

I wandered around until I found a wall clock: 7:45. Same time as at home. The Library had transported me through space but not time. It was early morning, before the first class started. I knew that once the bell rang and the kids scrambled to first period, I'd be out in the cold without a hall pass. I had to find out whatever I could before the halls emptied. Nothing like a little pressure.

I found a set of doors that led outside to a huge court-yard. The school building was three sides of a square, with the open side facing a road. The courtyard looked to be the main place where kids hung out. It was a big school, like mine. There had to be a few hundred kids waiting around for first period to start. I walked down several cement steps and wandered through the crowd, trying to get a feel for the place. It was nearly November and there was a definite chill in the air. I wished I'd brought a jacket.

The building was four stories and made of the same brown brick as the inside corridor walls. Imposing white columns in front gave it the feel of some important government building. If I had to guess, I'd say it was well over a hundred years old. A wrought iron fence with a wide-open gate closed off the courtyard from the road, where SUVs kept pulling up to drop off kids. Looking beyond the road, I saw nothing but trees. There wasn't a house or any other kind of building in sight. Coppell seemed like a rural school built out in the middle of nowhere.

The courtyard was packed. Some kids were talking in small groups, while others sat and read. A few tossed around a football.

I walked to the middle of the courtyard and did a three-sixty. In just a few minutes I had gotten a general sense of Coppell Middle School . . . and I still had no idea how to investigate the disruption.

A laugh went up from a group of kids crowded next to a far wall. Not knowing what else to do, I wandered over to see what the fun was.

What I found was not fun at all.

The kids formed a ring around a bench against the wall. Sitting on the bench and looking uncomfortable was a girl with long, wavy red hair. She hugged a backpack on her lap and stared straight at the ground, as though she wanted to be anywhere else. Sitting right next to her was the short thug from the bathroom. Nate.

"Anything," he said, laughing. "One word. Hello. Good-bye. Bite me. Anything!"

"Isn't 'bite me' two words?" one of his moron friends shouted out.

The kids laughed. The girl looked pained. She probably would have run off but she was trapped inside the circle.

Nate got to his feet and addressed the crowd, striding back and forth like he was a showman and the girl was part of a demonstration.

"I'll bet anybody," Nate announced boldly, "I can get her to talk."

"Yeah," some guy yelled. "She'll tell you to shut up!"

The kids all laughed.

"That would count!" Nate declared. "Who wants to bet?"

"She hasn't said a word in five years," one kid called out. "What makes you think you can get her to say something now?"

Nate swelled up his chest and smiled. "I can be very persuasive."

He spun around and looked down on the poor girl.

She looked as though she wanted to die. She seemed painfully shy . . . the perfect target for a bully like Nate.

I hate bullies. I believe I've made that perfectly clear.

"You got a great deal here, Kayla," Nate said quietly. "Whatever I make I'll split with you, seventy-thirty. I know you can talk, right? Or are you some kind of imbecile?"

My blood started to boil. I don't know who angered me more: Nate for being such a jackwagon, or the kids who thought he was funny.

Nate sat down next to Kayla again and leaned in, sticking his nose close to her ear.

She cowered, looking ready to cry.

"Is that the deal? Are you an idiot?" Nate asked with a snarl. "You could lose me a lot of money. Just say something."

That did it. Somebody had to stop this fool. I pushed my way through the crowd to get inside the circle, my eyes trained on Nate, ready to grab him by his worn hoodie and pull him away from the girl. At that moment I didn't care about fixing a disruption. This guy needed a pounding.

"Nate!" came an enraged voice.

I put on the brakes because I thought a teacher had arrived to break up the party. But it wasn't a teacher. It was another girl. She pushed her way through the crowd with as much purpose as I had, only she got to Nate first.

"Leave her alone!" she commanded furiously.

Nate jumped to his feet to face her.

"Butt out, Murcer," Nate barked.

The two stood nose to nose. I half expected Nate to take a swing at her. Or the other way around—that's how angry this girl looked. It seemed like things were going to get real nasty real fast, so the other kids moved away to give them space.

The girl was the same height as Nate. Her short blond hair and preppy plaid skirt and sweater made her look like the last person who would duke it out with a tough guy, but her attitude said otherwise. She was on fire.

"What is wrong with you?" she demanded angrily.

"What're you gonna do about it?" Nate replied. He was smug, but his cool had been shaken.

There was a long, tense moment while each waited for the other to make a move, when—

"Look out!" someone shouted.

All eyes went upward to see a large pane of glass falling straight toward the bench.

The blond girl reacted first. While everyone stood staring at the lethal blade, she shoved Nate and kept pushing him. Nate hit Kayla, and the three went tumbling, knocking the bench over and falling to the ground . . . as the huge glass pane hit the cement bench with an explosive crash.

That woke everybody up. Kids screamed in terror and dove away as a wave of broken glass washed over them. I turned and threw my arms up to protect my head but still felt the tiny pinpricks of a dozen little shards hitting my arms and neck as the shattered mass blew outward. The short, sharp sound the glass made when it exploded bounced back from the brick walls, followed by the tinkling of a million bits that hit the pavement where the kids had been standing.

The drama was over in an instant. Everyone stood frozen, probably in shock, while other kids ran up to see what had happened.

"I didn't do it!" a voice yelled down from above.

Standing inside the window frame where the glass had come from was one of Nate's goon friends. He peered out of the now empty frame with wide, frightened eyes.

"I swear!" he called down. "I was just walking by."

Someone pushed past me. It was Kayla. She'd finally gotten up the guts to run away. I guess near decapitation will do that.

The blond girl and Nate sat on the ground, covered in bits of broken glass. Both looked shell-shocked. Nobody else moved. It was as if they were all waiting for somebody to take charge and explain what had just happened.

The school bell rang.

It was exactly what the crowd needed to snap them back into normalcy. They quickly gathered up their books and packs and ran for the school building as they were programmed to do.

Nate and the blond girl finally got to their feet. They still looked shaken. I expected Nate to thank her for saving his life. He didn't. Instead, he pointed a threatening finger at her.

"Stay away from me, Ainsley, or you'll be sorry," he said with such venom that I truly believed he meant it. With one last glare, he took off for the front door of the school.

The girl, Ainsley, gingerly picked bits of glass from her sweater.

This was a girl I wanted to know.

I cautiously approached her.

"You okay?" I asked.

"Sure. It's just one more thing to go wrong around here."

"Yeah," I said. "I heard there's been a lot of strange stuff going on."

Teachers started flooding out of the school building and heading for the accident scene. I didn't want to be there when they arrived, so I walked away and motioned for Ainsley to follow me. Surprisingly, she did.

She stopped picking at glass, focused on me, and said, "I don't know you."

"Yeah, I'm, uh, I'm new. First day. My name's Marcus O'Mara."

"Ainsley Murcer," she said, and held out her hand to shake, very businesslike and efficient. "I'm the eighth-grade president."

"Of course you are," I said with a chuckle, and instantly regretted it.

She frowned. "What does that mean?"

"Nothing," I said quickly, covering. "You just seem like somebody who would be a class president. I mean, the way you stood up for that girl. Very cool."

The sound of far-off sirens intruded on our conversation.

"Fire department must be on their way," I said.

"They've been spending a lot of time here," Ainsley said. "They must be sick of making the trip. Then again, it's never been a false alarm."

"I don't have a schedule yet," I said. "I'm just kind of checking out classes. Would you mind if I tagged along with you today? I mean, who better to find out about the school from than the class president?"

Ainsley brightened at the idea. I had totally read her right. She was the kind of girl who knew everything about everything and loved to show that knowledge off.

"Sure," she said with a warm smile. "I should probably give the fire department a statement first."

"You think of everything, don't you?"

Ainsley shrugged. "I try."

"I'll wait by the door."

"Okay, you've got yourself an ambassador."

She gave me a satisfied smile and was about to head back to the accident scene, when she stopped and turned to me.

"Seriously, Marcus, with all that's been going on around here, I'm not so sure it's a good time for anybody to start at Coppell."

"I'll take my chances," I said.

"Brave guy," she said with another smile. "I like that."

She spun on her heel and jogged off.

47

I backed away, headed for the school entrance. I was proud of myself for coming up with a cover story to explain why I was there. Not that anybody would notice one extra kid. They had more important things on their minds . . . like a disaster that nearly killed three students. I'd been at Coppell for only ten minutes and I already sensed that Everett's instincts were right.

There was a disruption here. I was sure of it.

I had also stumbled on a couple of people who could very well be square in the middle of it. Nate was trouble and Kayla had issues. Were they victims or part of the disruption?

Better still, I had the eighth-grade class president to show me around.

Maybe Everett was right about something else too.

I might be good at this after all.

CHAPTER
4

Ainsley's first-period class was social studies, and it was definitely a social class.

"Why hasn't he been expelled?" one kid shouted as soon as Mr. Martin, the teacher, walked in. "The guy's a menace."

Another kid shouted, "It's not just him—it's his whole crew! You know they're the ones doing all this stuff."

"Who exactly are we talking about?" Martin asked innocently.

Most everyone shouted out, "Nate Christmas!"

The class went chaotic with everyone shouting out their opinions. Nobody was defending Nate.

I sat at a desk in the back row, trying to be invisible.

Ainsley was sitting quietly in the first row, looking straight ahead, her hands folded on her desk.

"All right, all right!" Martin called out, his hands raised, trying to quiet the class. "One at a time."

Martin was a young guy with longish blond hair that he kept sweeping out of his eyes. He wore jeans with a blue shirt, tucked in, and a thin tie. Unlike my social studies teacher at home, Mr. Winser, this guy looked fairly human. He wasn't getting all bent because the kids in the class were going out of their minds. He had a calm way about him that allowed for their anger to boil over while he still kept things in control.

"Parker," Martin called out, pointing to a girl in the third row.

"I saw Nate's friend Logan in the window right after the glass fell," she said. "He must have pushed it. They planned the whole thing."

The class chimed in with various shouts of agreement like "Yeah!" and "I saw him too!"

"That's a pretty serious accusation," Martin said, trying to sound evenhanded.

A girl in the front row shot to her feet. "I heard Nate was buying lighter fluid and matches at the 7-Eleven. Then the next day, there was a fire in the cafeteria kitchen. You can't tell me that's a coincidence."

Everyone grumbled in agreement.

"Noah," Martin said as he pointed to a guy near me who was waving his hand in the air, begging to be called on.

"Nate set off those firecrackers under the bleachers at the pep rally," Noah said. "And he's got a lot more than that. The guy has, like, an arsenal of explosives. He brags about it all the time. Cherry bombs, M-80s, you name it. That's why the bleachers fell down."

"Firecrackers don't cause bleachers to collapse," Martin said. "And nobody proved Nate set off the firecrackers."

"How can you defend him?" Parker shouted in frustration. "It's getting scary to come to school!"

"I'm defending someone who hasn't been proven guilty," Martin said. "Civics 101. Until the investigation plays out, we have to assume Nate is innocent. That's the way it works in this country."

Noah said, "Until he's proven guilty I think he should be thrown out of here. Or locked up. If the teachers don't do something, maybe us kids should."

"Yeah!" Parker chimed in. "Before somebody really gets hurt!"

Most kids liked that idea and chimed in with applause and whoops.

Martin held up his hands again to calm the class. "This isn't the Wild West, people. You're making an assumption of guilt based on incomplete evidence. Hear-say. Rumor. You're seeing the facts the way you want to see them, to support your own theories. What about the car that crashed through the window? How could Nate have done that? And when the power went out? Could a kid blow up a transformer?"

Nobody responded.

"What are you suggesting, Mr. Martin?" Ainsley said calmly, speaking for the first time. "Somebody has to be responsible for what's going on. If it isn't Nate, then who? Evil spirits?"

That got a couple of nervous chuckles.

Martin smiled patiently and said, "No, there's no boogeyman at Coppell."

He was right about that. The boogeyman was trapped in a metal box at the bottom of the Long Island Sound, thank you very much.

"I wouldn't be so sure about that," Ainsley said ominously.

"All I'm saying is we can't rush to judgment," Martin said. "We don't even know if these events are connected. It could all be a series of unfortunate coincidences. We'll get to the bottom of it soon enough. We just have to let the process play out."

"And hope nobody gets hurt in the meantime," Ainsley said.

That sobering thought left the class speechless.

Martin scanned the room and finally spotted me. "I see a new face in class."

Busted.

"Who might you be?" Martin asked.

All eyes went to me.

Showtime.

"My name's Marcus O'Mara. My family just moved here and I think I'll be going to Coppell. I'm not registered yet, so Ainsley is letting me follow her around to check the school out."

It was amazing how easily the lies flew out of my mouth. I suppose I should have felt guilty. I didn't. I was undercover.

"Well, Mr. O'Mara, have you heard much about the string of accidents we've had?"

"A little," I said. Lying again. I knew all about them. Maybe I had a future as an undercover cop. Or a spy. Or a politician.

"Coming from the outside, do you have any theories about what we're dealing with?" Martin asked.

"Not yet," I said. "But I'm working on it."

That got a chuckle out of some of the kids. They had no idea that it was the only totally honest thing I'd said.

"Well, best of luck, Mr. O'Mara. I hope you can solve our dilemma."

I hoped so too. More than he'd ever know.

Martin spent the rest of the class talking about ancient Rome and the construction of the Colosseum. It was actually kind of fun to be in a classroom and not have to worry about remembering anything the teacher was saying. I took the time to think, and to plan my next move.

The kids blamed Nate Christmas for all the dangerous doings. Ainsley was dead-solid certain it was him. Since she seemed to know everything about everything, I figured I should definitely consider the possibility that this was Nate's story. The real question was, why? Had he done something that caused the disruption? Or was he a victim?

Or was he just a plain old jerk?

As the class lecture went on, I kept my eye on Ainsley. She sat up straight, paying strict attention to Martin, as if whatever he was saying was the most important thing in the world. She took lots of notes too. I wondered if her parents put the same kind of pressure on her about school as Lu's parents did.

When class ended I walked with Ainsley through the crowded halls to her next class. Maybe I was imagining things, but I felt serious tension in the air. There wasn't the normal loud chatter when classes passed. It was like everyone was constantly glancing back over their shoulders, waiting for the next boom to be lowered.

"Why does everybody blame this Nate guy?" I asked Ainsley.

"Because he's a stupid thug," she replied with more than a drop of venom. "This is his first year here and he's already threatened to beat up half the student population. He's a bad apple and he's gotten other delinquents to join him. I'm the class president. I wish I could, like, expel him or something. This school was so awesome before he showed up."

"What is it you do as president?" I asked.

"Everything. I organize dances, plan fund-raisers, arrange pajama days, map out all our festivals, including the Halloween Fright Night dance and the Spring Fling party. I'm basically in charge of school spirit, which means I run the pep squad and the cheerleaders and arrange for our band to play at events and—"

"Whoa, okay. I get it. When do you sleep?"

"I don't" was her totally serious answer. "Not much, anyway."

We passed a row of lockers, where the girl Nate had been harassing that morning was getting her books.

"Hi, Kayla!" Ainsley called to her as we passed by.

Kayla gave her a weak smile and then buried her nose back in her locker.

"What's her deal?" I asked when we were out of earshot.

"She's shy," Ainsley said. "I mean, painfully so. I've known her for a couple of years and I've never heard her say a single word."

"Is she, like, special needs or something?" I asked.

"Not that I know of. She's in all the regular classes. But she doesn't have any friends. I looked it up once. Her silence has to do with extreme shyness. I've tried to get to know her, but it's hard when she won't give anything back."

"And you look out for her," I said.

"Sometimes, and today I nearly got killed because of it. It's just another reason for me to hate Nate Christmas."

I didn't know if I was any closer to figuring out whether Nate was responsible for the accidents, but he was definitely the most hated guy in school. I had to learn more about him, and I got my chance in Ainsley's next class, biology. When we walked in, I saw that Kayla was sitting near the back of the room. Seeing her made me laugh to myself. I was already getting to know this school and the kids. Instead of desks, there were tall stools and black-surfaced lab tables with built-in sinks and gas jets. There was no way I could blend into that crowd, so I walked right up to the teacher, a lady named

Miss Britton, and gave her the same bogus story about checking out the school before I transferred in.

"Then welcome to Coppell!" she said with a bright smile and a thick Southern accent that sounded more Georgia than Massachusetts. "Sit anywhere you'd like!"

I walked to the rear of the room and took the gunfighter's seat, the farthest seat back, so I could see the entire class. The stool I chose was close to the lab station where Ainsley sat. She was leaning over the table and talking to a friend, until Nate Christmas walked into the room.

Ainsley saw him and stiffened. She didn't even want to be in the same room as the guy—that's how much she hated him.

I glanced to Kayla. She kept her head buried in her biology book, like it was some kind of page-turning thriller.

Nate surveyed the room. When he focused on Ainsley, he tensed up as well. The little guy's jaw muscles worked as if he was holding in anger as he strode directly toward her lab table like a confident rooster.

Ainsley ignored him, keeping her eyes straight ahead.

A guy was sitting on the stool behind her. Nate went up to him, grabbed his shirt, and forcefully pulled him off the seat. The guy resisted until he saw who it was, then abruptly backed off and took another seat.

My pulse quickened again. I was beginning to see why everybody hated Nate Christmas.

Nate took the vacated stool a few feet behind Ainsley and moved it a little closer to her.

Nothing good was going to come of this.

Miss Britton's lecture was on algae, not exactly a fascinating subject under any circumstances. I was way more interested in Nate and Ainsley.

"You coming after me?" Nate whispered. He was being quiet enough so that Miss Britton couldn't hear, but Ainsley could. She sat up straight, as if his words had put her on full alert.

"I dare you," he growled in a low, menacing voice. "I want you to."

Everyone else's attention was on Miss Britton. There was only one other student aware of the low-key drama playing out.

Kayla. She sat at the lab table to our right. She was no longer focused on her book. Like me, she had her gaze fixed on Nate and Ainsley.

"You're telling everybody it's my fault, aren't you?" Nate said.

Ainsley never turned around. But it was clear that she heard every word he was saying, because she sat there as rigid as a mannequin. I wanted her to spin around and smack the guy. Or at least move to another seat. I thought about saying something, but I didn't belong there and didn't want to draw any attention to myself. That definitely ruled out my punching Nate in the head, which was what I really wanted to do. I had to sit there and take it, just like Ainsley. If her blood was boiling as hot as mine, I don't know how she kept from slugging him.

"Where do you get off blaming me anyway?" Nate asked. "You think you're something special. Trust me, you're not."

I heard a faint sound. It was like a gentle rattle. I took a quick look around but didn't see anything that could be making it. I thought maybe it was the ventilation system and tried to ignore it.

The lab table where Ainsley sat was near a wall and next to a long counter. Over the counter were shelves filled with glassware and bottles of . . . whatever. Science stuff.

"I didn't start this," Nate whispered. "This is all on you."

The rattling grew louder. It sounded like glass bottles were lightly tapping against one another. Kayla heard it too. She was no longer staring at Nate and Ainsley. Her gaze drifted to the counter and up to the shelf of bottles above it. I looked in the same direction and saw a row of brown bottles with stoppers and warning labels.

"You best keep looking over your shoulder," Nate said. "Or you won't see me coming."

The rattling got so loud that the entire class heard it, including Miss Britton. She stopped her lecture and looked around.

"Now, who is doing that?" she asked, annoyed.

CRACK!

One of the brown bottles on the shelf burst, sending clear liquid pouring onto the counter below. The sharp odor hit me instantly. It smelled like the strongest chlorine treatment you could ever put in a swimming pool. My eyes started watering and my nose burned.

"Look out!" Miss Britton shouted. "That's hydrochloric acid!"

Ainsley and Nate dove away. Other bottles on the shelf started shaking as if a mini-earthquake were centered directly under it. Many more bottles of acid were lined up, side by side. They all started to shake and bounce. If they broke and their contents splashed down, kids would get burned.

Over the shelf was a large silver showerhead, there for just such an emergency. We were told in science class that if you spilled something caustic, use the shower.

I figured this qualified as an emergency, so I dove for the metal chain next to the showerhead and yanked it. Water instantly sprang from the round showerhead, cascading down like a mini-rainstorm. It made a total mess, but when the water hit the counter, it diluted the acid enough that the smell went away almost entirely. The bottles stopped shaking too.

"Everybody back off!" Miss Britton yelled, losing her cool. "Don't touch anything."

I backed away quickly. I didn't want to be splashed by acid, diluted or not.

The rest of the class was huddled together against the opposite wall, watching in stunned wonder.

"How did this happen?" Miss Britton shouted. "Who did this?"

There were no answers because nobody knew. I had been sitting right there and I didn't know. Nobody had touched anything. It was as if the bottle just decided to break on its own.

The kids looked shell-shocked. There was no screaming or sobbing. I guess they were getting used to having strange things like this happen.

Ainsley stood in front of the others as if to shield them. She stood defiantly straight and tall, as if to say she would not be defeated by a little bit of acid.

Nate, on the other hand, looked pretty shaken. He

had run all the way to the front of the room to escape the acid and was checking his clothes for burns.

The only kid who wasn't staring at the mess was Kayla. She sat in the back of the room, leaning against the wall, twirling her long hair around a finger.

One good thing came from the scary event. It helped me narrow down my search for the cause of the disruption. I felt pretty certain that whoever or whatever was causing it was in that room. All I had to do was figure out what it was.

Yeah. That.

CHAPTER
5

NOBODY WAS BURNED. No real damage was done other than the kids being kept on edge, wondering when the next dangerous accident would happen, and whether they might be the one caught in it. They had been lucky up till then, but how long would that luck last?

Everett was sitting in his usual spot at the circulation desk, glasses down on his nose, reading from the red book that held the story about Coppell Middle School.

"It's a disruption, all right," I declared. "There's nothing right about anything that's going on at that crazy school."

I had left Coppell the same way I arrived . . . through the janitor's closet in the boys' room. It was weird to think that getting around that way was feeling less, well, weird.

"Any theories on who might be causing it?" Everett asked as he skimmed the new entries.

"Lots of the kids are blaming a weasel named Nate Christmas. But it doesn't make sense that Nate could be doing all this stuff. It's not like he's got some strange powers. At least not that I know of."

"He's the only suspect?" Everett asked.

"Maybe. There's a girl named Kayla who's been square in the middle of a bunch of the events. But I can't talk to her because she doesn't speak. At all. To anybody. I guess she hasn't said a word in years."

Everett raised an eyebrow.

"She could be worth pursuing," he said as he scanned the book's pages. "There has to be a story there."

The spirits who wrote the stories had already documented in the red book everything that happened. All Everett had to do was read to get caught up. Hard to believe, but that was starting to feel normal to me too.

"What d'ya plan on doing next?" Everett asked.

I headed for the door that led back to reality. My reality.

"I want to find out more about those kids," I said. "But I'll need help."

"Lu and Theo?" Everett asked.

"Yeah. I made friends with the girl who's president of the eighth grade. She can open doors for us."

I walked quickly toward the exit.

"Marcus?" Everett called.

I turned back to him but kept walking.

"Yeah?"

"Exceptional work, lad. Your father couldn't have done any better himself."

His words meant more to me than he knew. My whole life I'd wondered if I was anything like my biological parents. Turns out that I was. At least in the sleuthing department.

Or maybe Everett only said that because he knew exactly how much it would mean to me and wanted to make sure I'd come back.

"Yeah, well, I haven't done anything yet," I said, and went for the door.

I pushed the exit door open and stepped into . . .

. . . my bathroom at home. No sooner did I close the door behind me than somebody knocked on it. I pulled it open expecting to see Everett with some last-second thought. Instead, I was jarred to see my dad standing in our upstairs hallway.

It took a couple of seconds for me to reset my brain and register how that was possible. There were some things about the Library I was still having trouble getting used to.

"You feeling okay?" he asked with a worried frown.

His question threw me.

"Uh, yeah. Why?"

"Because you ran up here like you were going to explode. I wanted to make sure you weren't puking your guts out. Or something."

Oh. Right. I had left my parents at breakfast and ran upstairs when I felt the Paradox key grow warm. Even though I had been at Coppell Middle School for a couple of hours, I returned home at the exact second I'd left. This time-displacement thing was yet another weirdness that needed some getting used to.

"Yeah, I'm fine," I said. "False alarm. Gas . . . I guess."

I flushed the toilet for effect.

"Oh. Good. Well, I'm glad you're going to give some thought to what we suggested."

"About what?" I asked.

He gave an exasperated sigh. "About looking into joining some extracurricular activities."

Oh. Right. The domestic conflict of the day.

I laughed.

"Why's that funny?" Dad asked, perturbed.

"Sorry, it's not. Don't worry. I'll come up with something. See you tonight."

I pushed past my dad and headed out of the bathroom, still laughing to myself. My parents wanted me to find some kind of extracurricular interest. They had no idea I was going on adventures that made joining some lame school club seem like a joke. The trick was to get them off my back so I wouldn't have to actually join some after-school thing, because I was way too busy traveling through different dimensions.

The next morning, following a full day of school and a solid night's sleep, I went right back to Coppell through the Library to continue the investigation. I waited until then because I didn't want to crash and burn by living through too many thirty-six-hour days. Though my normal life went on hold and didn't unfreeze until I got back home, my body kept going the whole time. I was still living and breathing when I was in a story, so I had to be careful not to spend too many hours in the Library or I really would end up like Rip Van Winkle.

At least on this trip I wasn't alone.

"Marvelous!" Theo exclaimed while gazing at the ancient brick school building. "I wouldn't be surprised if some of the original structure dated back to the 1800s."

"Old" was Lu's simple appraisal.

"Everett hasn't forgotten about your stories," I said.

"He's been looking, but there are a lot of books back there."

"Maybe there's nothing to find," Theo said hopefully. "We may not be going through disruptions after all."

"Maybe," I said. "But if you are, he'll find the stories. Or I will, if I have to look through every book myself."

Lu gave me a big smile and said, "Like you'd do that."

"Okay, maybe not, but I trust Everett. He's got a lot more time to look than I do."

"I get it. Let's worry about one story at a time," Lu said. "What do we do first?"

"There are three kids I want to know more about," I said. "I'll go for that d-bag Nate Christmas. He's public enemy number one."

"How could one kid do all of those things?" Lu asked, skeptically. "He may be a foul ball, but he's not magical. Or is he?"

"I don't know. Maybe. Everett said people sometimes get trapped in situations they don't understand because there's nothing logical about them."

"Well, that's pretty scary," Theo said.

"Yeah, Theo's worst nightmare," Lu said. "Stuck in a world with no logic. It would make his Spock brain explode."

"I'm sure it wouldn't bother you," Theo shot back.

"Seeing as you don't understand much about science anyway."

"I got a couple of lousy C's!" Lu exclaimed. "That doesn't make me an idiot."

"No, just average."

"Stop!" I shouted. "Can we focus, please? Theo, try to meet that girl Kayla. She was right in the middle of most of the incidents. It could be a coincidence, but you never know. She won't talk to you, but maybe you can get a feel for what she's all about."

"I'll try," Theo said. "I'm quite perceptive."

"Yeah, and it's not like you know how to talk to girls anyway," Lu said dismissively.

Theo scowled at her.

Lu smiled.

"What about me?" she asked.

"Find Ainsley Murcer. She runs this place and knows everything about everything. She might have seen things she didn't even realize she was seeing. You'll get along with her. You two are alike."

"But I'm an original," Lu said, aghast.

"I don't mean *exactly* alike. Jeez, just talk to her. If anybody asks why you're here, tell them you're new. That's worked for me."

"Maybe we should say we're all from the same

family," Lu suggested. "A white guy, an Asian girl, and a black guy—that's not suspicious at all."

"Yeah, don't do that," I said firmly. "It won't be a problem. The adults here are so spun around by what's happening they're not going to care about a few extra kids wandering around. Learn what you can and meet back here when the bell rings before first period."

"Marcus?" Theo said. "I'm feeling rather anxious about this."

"It's okay," I said. "They're normal kids. I think. But stay alert: you never know when something might fall on your head."

"That doesn't make me any less anxious," Theo said as he glanced to the sky, expecting something to be headed his way.

"No sweat," Lu said with confidence. "We beat the boogeyman. This'll be cake."

The three of us walked through the wrought iron gates and entered the early-morning bustle of the courtyard. I scanned the crowd, looking for our targets. It was as hectic as the day before, with kids being dropped off and hanging out until first period.

"There," I said. "That's Ainsley."

She was sitting at a table, working intently on something, papers spread out in front of her.

"She doesn't look anything like me," Lu said, annoyed.

"I didn't say she . . . oh, never mind, just go!"

Lu locked her eyes on Ainsley and went straight for her.

"What does Kayla look like?" Theo asked. "And in spite of what I just said about my superior perceptive abilities, how am I supposed to get information from a girl who doesn't speak?"

"Because of what you tell me at least three times a day."

"What's that?"

"You're smart. There she is."

I pointed at Kayla, who was sitting by herself on a bench just inside the fence. After nearly getting sliced by a falling sheet of glass, she probably didn't want to be anywhere near the school building.

Theo took a deep, nervous breath and said, "Wish me luck."

He took off, headed for Kayla.

On my own again, I went looking for the infamous Nate Christmas.

I found him and a couple of his pals in a far corner of the courtyard, keeping to themselves. Or maybe everybody else was steering clear. The three of them were in a circle, kicking around a soccer ball.

"Hey, you okay?" I asked him as I strolled up.

He gave me a quick, dismissive look and said, "What're you talking about?"

"The acid. In science. You get burned?"

I knew he wasn't hurt, but I needed some way to open up a conversation.

"Oh yeah," he said, looking at his friends. "Clark Kent here saved the day."

"It was weird how that happened," I said. "Nobody was close enough to the bottles to knock 'em over."

"Yeah, almost as weird as you spying on us in the bathroom, perv."

"I wasn't spying," I said, taking a deep breath to keep from letting him get to me. "But a lot of strange things have been happening here. Any idea why?"

Nate kicked the soccer ball hard, sending it sailing halfway across the courtyard.

"Hey!" one of his friends yelled angrily and went after it.

Nate walked up to me, getting uncomfortably close, and looked me square in the eye.

"You think everything's my fault too?" he snarled.

I felt his hot breath on my chin, but there was no way I'd back down from this munchkin bully, so I stood my ground and locked eyes with him.

"Nah, I'm just worried about you, chief," I said.

"Worried? Why?"

"Seems like you're always there when something goes wrong. Maybe somebody's got it out for you. Do you have any enemies . . . Nate?"

There was a subtle shift in his gaze, as if I'd told him something he hadn't thought of before. It lasted only a second before he locked back on me.

"Nah, everybody loves me," he said with a twisted grin. "What about you? Maybe you're the one who should be worried."

"I think we all have to worry a little," I said. "Be careful, chief. People are watching."

I turned my back on the guy and walked away. I wanted to make him nervous. If he thought people were circling him and about to close in, he might make a mistake that would tip his hand. It was the only thing I could think of doing.

I looked around for Lu and Theo and saw that they were with Ainsley and Kayla. Those guys were good. I knew I could rely on them. Later, I read about the details of their encounters.

WHILE MARCUS WAS SPEAKING with Nate, Lu marched right up to Ainsley and stood over her.

"Hi, my name's Annabella. Marcus O'Mara says you're the one who knows everything about this school."

Lu always got right to the point.

Ainsley looked up at her with a big, welcoming smile.

"Well, I don't know if I know everything, but pretty darn close. You have a pretty name. Are you new too?"

Lu sat down across from her.

"Yup. What're you working on?"

"The Halloween dance is tomorrow night. Fright Night. I've got to keep track of all the decoration and food bills for the PTA."

"Wow, that's pretty . . . adult of you," Lu said with genuine awe. "That's a lot of work."

"You have no idea," Ainsley said with a sigh. "Nobody volunteers to do anything, so I end up doing it all."

"And you still have time for schoolwork?" Lu asked.

"Sure. Late at night. If I don't keep getting perfect grades, my parents will make me give everything else up, and I don't want that to happen. The school would fall apart."

"My parents are the same way!" Lu exclaimed. "I'm getting a C in science and I'm afraid to tell them because they'll freak."

"I hear you, but you have to tell them," Ainsley said. "Hiding stuff makes it so much worse."

"I'm not so sure about that. Have you ever told your parents when you messed something up?"

"Sure. Not that it happens a lot, to be honest, but I tell them. They get it. Truth is, they give me a harder time when I'm doing okay. That's when they really push for me to do more. But when something doesn't work out, they back off and give me a little slack."

Lu let the words sink in. "That's pretty cool."

"The pressure can get intense, but I'm on top of everything. Most of the time." The two chuckled like they were old friends.

"I heard there have been a lot of accidents around school," Lu said. "What's going on?"

Ainsley's expression turned cold.

"Nate Christmas, that's what's going on," she said.

"Really? How can one kid do all that stuff?"

"Who knows? But he's got a whole posse to help him," Ainsley said with disdain. "He's bound to mess up eventually. He'll get caught. I'd love to be the one to catch him."

"I hope you do," Lu said.

Lu had no trouble getting to know her subject.

Theo, on the other hand, was having a harder time. For a few minutes, he watched Kayla work on her iPad as she sat alone on the end of the bench. No other kid went near her. It was like she was radioactive. Theo braced himself, gathered his nerve, and stepped up to her.

"Hi," he said brightly. "Mind if I sit here?"

Kayla looked up at him with no expression, then went back to her iPad.

Theo sat down a safe distance away, putting his backpack on the ground next to the bench.

"My name's Theo," he said. "I'm new here."

Kayla didn't look at him. Or respond.

"What's your name?"

Still no response.

"Wait, I know who you are. Kayla, right?"

Kayla stiffened but didn't look up.

"My friend Marcus told me about you. He's new too. But it's not like we knew each other before or came from the same school. Oh no, we've never met. I'm not even sure why I remember his name. He's not really a friend. I'm not even sure if his name is Marcus. Is it?"

Theo was running off at the mouth and getting zero reaction from Kayla. Desperate to come up with another way to break through Kayla's shell, he forced himself to shut up and sit in silence for a few seconds.

"It's not fun being new," he finally said. "Everything's so strange. I feel like everybody's sizing me up. Doesn't help being black either. Just makes me stand

76

out even more. It's weird being in such a huge group of people and feeling totally alone. Makes me want to go hide somewhere."

Kayla looked up and they made eye contact. Theo gave her a smile and a shrug. Kayla looked back at her iPad.

Her slight thaw gave Theo the confidence to try again.

"I don't have a lot of friends at my school," Theo said. "My old school, I mean. Kids think I'm a little strange. I don't think I am, but what I think doesn't count. I do have two good friends, though. That's all you need. One or two people who watch out for you and don't try to make you into something you're not. The trick is to find friends like that."

Kayla kept her eyes on her iPad.

Theo waited, hoping she would give him a clue that she had actually heard him.

"Well, thanks for listening," he said with another shrug. "Sorry to lay all of that on you."

He moved to get up, but Kayla's hand shot out and grabbed his arm, stopping him.

Theo's heart raced. Was she going to say something? He looked down at her as she held out her iPad for him to look at. She had typed something using the Notebook app.

Theo read aloud: "'What you think counts for a lot. I hope you make new friends here.'"

Kayla offered Theo a small smile.

Theo beamed.

"Thanks, Kayla. I appreciate that."

Kayla pulled the iPad back and looked down at it again. Interaction over.

"Hopefully I'll see you around," Theo said, then got up and strolled away.

We hadn't solved anything yet, but at least we were making ourselves part of this school and learning more of its secrets. But was that enough? Didn't seem so. The bell was about to ring and the three of us were going to have to figure out where to go until lunchtime, when we could blend in again.

"Hi, Ainsley," I said as I stepped up to the table where she sat with Lu. "I see you met my friend Lu—I mean, Annabella."

"She's great," Ainsley said in such a perky way I think she really meant it and wasn't just being nice. "I wish she had gotten here sooner—I could have really used the help. What do you say, Lu? Would you give me a hand sometimes? It'll be fun!"

Ainsley looked to Lu hopefully, waiting for an answer.

"Uh, sure," Lu said tentatively. "I need to get registered and set up first, though."

"No problem!" Ainsley exclaimed. "You can still help me with the dance tomorrow night. There are a million things I haven't even gotten to yet."

Lu gave me a helpless look, and was rescued by Theo, who ran up to join us.

"Success!" he exclaimed. "I made contact and actually got her to—"

"Uh, Theo, this is Ainsley."

Theo was confused that I had cut him off, then focused on Ainsley and realized he had to be careful about what he said.

"Oh! Hi, I'm Theo."

"You're transferring too?" Ainsley asked. "Coppell is suddenly getting very popular."

"Hey, look," Lu said.

We all looked at where she was pointing to see Kayla headed our way, carrying Theo's backpack.

"Oh man! I forgot it," Theo said.

"Kayla's bringing it to you?" Ainsley asked with surprise. "I . . . I . . . wow."

Theo shot me a smug look.

Kayla made her way through the crowd, headed straight for Theo.

Theo moved to meet her and . . .

. . . Nate appeared from behind Kayla, pushing his way through a crowd of kids to get to her.

"Uh-oh," I said. "Here we go again."

Nate had his eyes locked on Kayla, no doubt ready to harass her again to try and get her to say a few words so he could win his cruel bet.

"Hey, Kayla!" Nate yelled.

Kayla froze. A moment before she had appeared relaxed and almost happy to be bringing the backpack to Theo. Now it was like she had been hit with a jolt of electricity. She tensed up, her shoulders hunched, and her face fell.

"Not this time," I said, and started forward to head Nate off.

I had barely taken a step when I caught movement out of the corner of my eye. It was subtle and quick, but I was in a perfect position to see it.

Ainsley was sitting at the table next to me. Her hand flashed up as if to gesture *Stop!*

An instant later, a large metal trash can flipped over and fell directly in front of Nate. It happened so fast that Nate didn't have time to dodge it. He tripped over the heavy container and somersaulted forward, landing on his head.

Everyone laughed as Nate tumbled to the ground

and the can rolled over him. I would have laughed too, if not for what I had seen a second before.

Kayla started moving again. She dropped the backpack at Theo's feet, then hurried past him, headed for the school.

"Uh, thanks," Theo said.

The bell rang. The show was over. Everyone started for the front doors.

Ainsley quickly gathered her papers.

"What just happened?" Lu asked, stunned.

I kept watching Ainsley. She didn't even bother to put her papers in her pack, just jammed them under one arm. She wanted to be out of there. Fast.

I was the only one who had seen what she did.

"Ainsley?" was all I could manage to get out.

She ignored me and took off.

Nate got to his feet, acting all cool as if he had meant to trip and fall down like a fool. He brushed himself off and looked around to see who was watching.

Nobody was. Nobody cared that he had taken a fall or whether he was okay.

He headed for the school, glaring at the kids he walked past as if daring them to laugh.

"That was . . . odd," Theo said.

"Tell me about it," I said. "Change of plans. Let's get back to the Library."

C H A P T E R

6

"The trash can flew out of nowhere!" Lu exclaimed. "Like it had a mind of its own."

"I saw it too," Theo added. "I'm having trouble believing it, but I saw it."

I felt the heat of Everett's thoughtful gaze on me. He was trying to make sense of what had happened, the same as we were. He looked at the book in his hand and read:

> With a wave of her hand, a small gesture that went unnoticed by most everyone there, Ainsley seemed to command the metal container to fall to the ground directly in the path of the oncoming Nate, causing him to stumble over it, which allowed the Eggers girl to escape.

Everett looked back to me and said, "Is that how you saw it?"

I paced, trying to put my mind back in the moment to remember exactly what had happened.

"I think so," I said. "I mean, her hand came up like she was waving at Nate or something. A second later, the garbage can flipped over right in front of him. It could have been a coincidence."

"Sure," Lu shot back sarcastically. "A mini-tornado could have whipped through at that exact moment. I totally get that."

"So what really happened?" Theo asked. "Did Ainsley do it?"

All eyes went to Everett. He had been intently reading the account of what had happened like a scholar working through a complicated math problem. He glanced back at a few pages, then took off his glasses and rubbed his eyes.

"Did Ainsley do it?" Everett repeated. "Could be. But if so, the more important question is *why* did she do it? Let's suppose this is Ainsley's story. That gives us two possibilities. If she's intentionally causing all this mayhem, it must be for a reason. You don't often see mischief being done just for mischief's sake."

"She doesn't seem like somebody who causes problems," I said. "She's more of a fixer."

"Maybe she's a really good actress," Theo offered. "She could be fooling everybody."

"What's the second possibility?" Lu asked.

"She may be causing all the trouble . . . and not know it," Everett said.

"Uh . . . what?" Lu said, befuddled.

Everett motioned to the aisles of books. "These shelves are filled with stories about people caught in supernatural dilemmas. Ninety-nine times out of a hundred they brought it on themselves and didn't realize what they'd done until it was too late. Ainsley may be hiding something, or she may have no idea why it's happening. Either way, we have to find the reason for it. It's the only way to finish the story before something truly horrible happens."

"So what do we do?" Lu asked.

There was a long silence that I hoped Everett would fill with some wise advice.

He didn't.

So I did.

"Go to school," I said to Lu and Theo. "Our school. Both of you."

"What about you?" Theo asked.

"I'm going back to Coppell."

"No," Lu commanded. "Not by yourself. We want to help."

"You will," I said. "As soon as you leave the Library, I'll be right behind you. The only difference is I'll have gone back to Coppell for a while."

"I don't follow that," Theo said.

"It's true," Everett said. "When you step out of the Library, you'll be returning home at the exact second you left. Since you all came here at the same time, that means Marcus will as well, even if he goes back into the story first."

"This is making my head hurt," Lu said.

"It's easier for one of us to blend in at that school than all three," I said. "I'll talk to Ainsley and try to figure out what she knows. Or doesn't know. If I need you I'll come back and get you. Either way I'll be right behind you."

Theo and Lu didn't look too happy about leaving me alone.

"Go ahead, you two," Everett said. "Marcus will be right behind you . . . after a fashion."

"You better be," Lu said with authority.

She spun and headed for the exit.

Theo didn't move.

"You shouldn't go back there by yourself," he said.

"It's okay. This makes sense."

"None of this makes sense," he said with frustration. "Whether Ainsley is meaning to do these things or not, it's dangerous. You have to be careful."

"You know I will."

"I don't know that at all," Theo said.

He gave up arguing and followed Lu toward the exit.

"See you in a couple of seconds," I called after them.

Lu shook her head, bewildered. "Yeah, and how odd is that?"

She pushed the door open, and after one last worried look back at me, the two left.

"He's right, you know," Everett said. "Things are getting worse. I'm afraid it's only a matter of time before something tragic happens."

"So I shouldn't be hanging around here talking to you," I said, and started for the door that led into the story.

"Wait, there's something you haven't considered."

"Do I want to know what it is?" I asked.

"Probably not. I'm not saying there's a connection, mind you. We don't know yet, but it seems a wee bit of a coincidence that tomorrow night is Samhain."

"Sow-*what*?"

"The correct pronunciation is 'Sow-en.' It's one of the oldest sabbats, or holy days, on the calendar. It marks the changing of the seasons from light to dark. The ancient Celts looked upon it as the day when winter began. It's also the moment when the veil between this world and the next is at its thinnest."

"Never heard of it," I said.

"Why, sure you have. You just call it something else entirely: Halloween."

My stomach sank. "Oh jeez, that's right. But that's just folklore, right?"

"Sure it is," Everett said. "Just like the Boggin."

"So what does Halloween have to do with any of this?"

"Can't say that I know," Everett said. "I'll keep searching through the books. But like I said, disruptions happen for a reason. To think it's a coincidence that all this is happening during the run-up to All Hallows' Eve could be a dangerous mistake."

I wanted to scream.

"Swell," I said with true frustration. "First the boogeyman, now spooky-dooky Halloween. Are any of these unfinished stories *not* about ancient myths?"

Everett chuckled. "Stop your bellyaching. The beauty of these so-called myths is they give us some history to refer to. Otherwise we'd be relying on nothing but guesswork. The stories with no history are far tougher to crack."

"I guess," I said. "But I'd rather not be dealing with a disruption on the spookiest day of the year."

"I hear ya. Theo gave you wise advice, lad. Be careful."

I headed toward the exit. Or the entrance. Or

whatever the heck it was that would get me back into the story.

"And be wary of that Ainsley girl," Everett called out. "She may not be what she seems."

With too many mysteries flying around in my head, I left the Library and made my way back to Coppell Middle School through the usual route . . . the janitor's closet in the boys' room. A quick glance at a clock in the hall showed me it was still first period. Ainsley was in social studies class. I hurried through the empty corridors of the old school, hoping I wouldn't be stopped by a teacher demanding to see a hall pass. I got to the classroom and looked through the window of the closed door to see two things:

Mr. Martin was lecturing.

And Ainsley's desk was empty.

That was bad. Ainsley wasn't the type to miss class. A slight tickle of a warning nudged the most paranoid corner of my brain. Where was she? I decided to be bold and go to the school office. Why not? The worst thing they could do was kick me out for trespassing. I marched right up to the desk like I belonged and waved to a lady wearing an old-fashioned green tracksuit who looked like she'd worked there forever. Her permanent scowl said she wasn't particularly happy about it either.

I gave her a big, polite smile and said, "Excuse me. I

came from Mr. Martin's social studies class. He wants to know why Ainsley Murcer isn't there."

The cranky old lady frowned and squinted at me as if trying to figure out who the heck I was. The tiny curls of her short gray hairdo were almost as tight and gray as her expression.

"He was worried about her," I added, trying to get her attention off me and onto Ainsley.

"She went to the nurse," the woman said. "Wasn't feeling well."

"Okay, thanks," I said, backing toward the door.

"Wait, what's your name—?"

"Thank you!" I called, and bolted before she could nail me.

The nurse. Where was the nurse's office? I scanned the corridor and saw a series of doors to my right. I was flying by the seat of my pants. I wasn't even sure what I'd say to Ainsley if I found her.

Sure enough, the nurse's office was only a few doors down from the main office. Before I could chicken out, I walked right in to see a much younger woman than the lady in green sitting behind a desk. She was on the telephone and held up one finger to ask me to wait a second.

I took a peek further into the office and saw that several yards beyond the desk, somebody was sitting in a cubicle with the curtain drawn. Was it Ainsley?

The nurse hung up the phone and gave me a sweet smile.

"What can I do for you?" she asked.

"Mr. Martin sent me. He wanted to know how Ainsley was doing."

I kept stealing glances toward the drawn curtain, hoping to see if it was her or not.

"She's fine," the nurse said. "She called her mother to come pick her up."

"Who is that?" came a voice from behind the curtain. It was Ainsley.

"Mr. Martin sent someone to see how you're doing," the nurse called to her.

Ainsley pulled the curtain back a few inches and peeked out at me.

"I want to talk to him," she said.

My heart leapt. I hadn't expected this to be so easy.

The nurse gave me an uncertain look. I wasn't sure if it was because she didn't know who I was, or because she wasn't supposed to let boys visit girls in her domain.

"Are you feeling better?" the nurse asked.

"Not really. But I want the company."

The nurse shrugged and motioned for me to go in.

"Keep the curtain open," she warned, but with a wink and a smile.

"No problem," I said.

What did she think we were going to do? Make out?

I rounded the desk and walked the ten yards down the corridor to Ainsley's cubicle. I gently pushed the curtain aside and looked in to see her sitting on a cot, leaning against the wall and gazing absentmindedly out the window.

"You okay?" I asked.

She shrugged.

I had known Ainsley Murcer only a short time, but it was long enough to know she was not the type to be daydreaming and looking out the window during all-important school hours.

I glanced back to the nurse to find her watching me. When our eyes met, she turned away quickly as if she didn't want me to think she was being nosy, even though she was totally being nosy.

"You sick?" I asked Ainsley as I stepped into the cubicle.

Ainsley chuckled as if I had asked a stupid question.

"Maybe," she said. "I don't know. I just want to go home."

I sat down in a folding chair across from her. This was going to be tricky. I wanted her to tell me what was going on, but I didn't want to push so hard that she would think I suspected her of anything. My experience with the Boggin had taught me to be careful about who to trust.

"You saw it, didn't you?" she asked.

"Saw what?" I asked innocently, though I knew exactly what she was talking about.

She didn't answer the question. She knew that I knew.

"I've been thinking," she said dreamily. "About all the things that have been happening. The falling window, the fire in the cafeteria, the bleachers collapsing—everything."

"What about 'em?"

"I've been blaming Nate because I saw him in all those places. But the only reason I saw him was because I was there too. Maybe none of it was Nate's fault."

"Are you saying it was you?" I asked tentatively.

Ainsley finally looked at me. She had tears in her eyes.

"I don't know," she said, her voice cracking. "I don't think so. But it can't all be coincidence."

"But it's not like you knocked out the window or spilled the acid. How could you have done any of that?"

Ainsley wiped away her tears.

"This is going to sound crazy," she said.

"Go for it. I'm good with crazy."

"Every time something happened, I was like, I don't

know, emotional. I was upset. Or angry. Or excited. Like today. I saw Nate headed for Kayla and my heart started pounding. I wanted to jump out of that chair and tackle him. Instead, I just . . ."

She couldn't finish the thought.

"Instead you used your emotions to fling a garbage can at him?" I asked.

"Yes! I mean, I don't know. I told you it was crazy."

She looked back out the window and her expression changed instantly. She sat bolt upright, her eyes fixed on something outside.

I looked out the window and saw it.

A big white dog—or was it a wolf?—stood on the grass about ten yards away.

The sight was so out of place it made me catch my breath. The animal was snowy white, with a narrow, diamond-shaped black blaze between its eyes. There wasn't an owner in sight, and since classes were going on, no kids were around to see it.

The animal stood at attention, its gaze focused directly on Ainsley.

I looked back and forth between the two as if witnessing a staring contest.

Ainsley couldn't take her eyes off it.

"Tell me that's your dog," I said.

She didn't answer, or break her stare.

"It doesn't have a collar," I said. "It could be a wild—"

Ainsley jumped to her feet and hurried out of the cubicle.

"Uh . . . whoa. W-w-wait!" I stammered, and followed her.

She walked quickly past the nurse, headed for the door.

"Your mother's not here yet," the nurse called.

Ainsley ignored her and sped out the door.

"Guess she's feeling better," I said to the nurse with a helpless shrug, and followed Ainsley out.

"I'll write a pass!" the nurse called.

Too late. We were gone.

Ainsley hurried down the long corridor, away from the school's main entrance.

"Where are you going?" I called.

Ainsley's answer was to pick up the pace. There was no way I was going to let her out of my sight, so I kept up. She went straight for a fire exit halfway down the corridor, and blasted outside.

I followed her to see . . .

. . . the dog standing there, waiting, as if it knew Ainsley would be coming out that way.

The beast was big. Scary big. It had to be over a hundred twenty pounds. Its thick white coat glowed in the early-morning sunlight, making the black blaze between its eyes look even more dark and menacing.

"Is it a dog or a wolf?" I asked.

The dog—that's what I'll call it, because I really hoped it wasn't a wolf—turned and trotted off.

"Stay here, Marcus," Ainsley said.

"Why?" I asked. "Where are you going?"

Her answer was to take off after the dog.

I let her go for a few seconds, then followed.

The animal trotted along steadily, keeping about ten yards ahead. It never looked back to see if we were following, but it didn't try to lose us either. It moved with confidence, as if it knew exactly where it was going. It always cracks me up when animals do that, like they have an important meeting to get to or something.

But this time I wasn't laughing. Whatever mission the big dog was on, it couldn't be good.

It rounded the corner of the brick building and kept going. Coppell Middle School was built on the edge of deep, thick woods. We followed the dog across a huge parking lot, snaking between parked cars until we hit a wide stretch of grass that bordered the asphalt and separated the school property from the woods.

The white dog kept moving. It trotted across the grass, shot between two trees, and was gone.

"You sure you want to follow it in there?" I asked Ainsley.

I might as well not have been there. She totally ignored me and entered the woods, her attention laser-locked on the dog.

This had gotten seriously weird. I looked back over the sea of cars to the school building. The school had doors. Lots of them. The woods didn't. If I had to get out of there in a hurry, there would be no escaping back into the Library. Whatever waited in there, I'd have to deal with it. I told Theo I'd be careful. I lied. Something strange was going on, and strange had become my business. So I blew past the first row of trees and entered the dark pine forest.

It was like stepping into dusk as the temperature instantly dropped twenty degrees. The ground was covered by a vast carpet of dry pine needles that had fallen from the dozens of trees that stood everywhere. Going by their size, the trees had to be hundreds of years old. Way older than the school. They stretched to the sky, where their branches grew together to create a thick canopy that blocked out most of the sunlight. And warmth.

The sudden drop in temperature wasn't the only thing that sent chills up my spine.

The white dog-wolf padded silently ahead, weaving

between the trees, headed deeper into the woods. Its white fur stood out against the dark foliage, making it look like a fleeting ghost. Stranger still, the normally buttoned-up and in-control Ainsley Murcer had fallen under its spell.

I, on the other hand, was under no such spell and was getting nervous. There were still no answers as to why Ainsley may have caused all those accidents. If she was telling the truth, she had no idea what was happening and had no control over whatever power might have caused the damage. That only made me more nervous. We were in the middle of the woods. I didn't want to be caught out there alone if those powers decided to show up again and things started flying around.

The woods became dense as we left the pines and entered a stretch filled with thick bushes and white birch trees. The dog skirted the trees easily, but they slowed Ainsley and me down as we picked our way through. I kept hoping she'd look at me and snap out of it, but her attention was locked on the dog.

As we broke out from a thick stand of bushes, I saw movement in the air. It was a bird. I caught only a quick glimpse as it flew from one tree into the branches of another, but I saw enough to know that it was pure white. And big. At first I thought it was a seagull, but I was pretty sure we weren't anywhere near the ocean.

I stared at the spot in the tree where it had disappeared, but there was nothing more to see, so I kept moving . . . as another bird swooped by from behind, nearly grazing my head before sailing up toward the overhead canopy of leaves.

I got a better look at this one. It was as big as the other bird, and also pure white. It looked like a crow. Or a raven. I'm not sure which is which. But I'd never heard of a white raven. It sure sounded like one, though. It let out a quick *caw* before disappearing into the same tree the first one had flown into. I couldn't say why the birds gave me the creeps, but something about them wasn't right. I glanced up and around at the other trees that surrounded us, waiting for another bird to buzz by.

Ainsley, on the other hand, had zero interest in the birds. She never stopped moving and was now twenty yards ahead of me. I had to run to catch up, jumping over fallen trees and moss-covered rocks.

The white dog was still ahead of her. Without hesitation, it scampered into a dense line of deep green leafy bushes. Up until that point it had dodged around every obstruction it came upon. This time it barreled straight into the wall of green that stretched on either side of us like a tall barricade that surrounded a fort.

Ainsley followed right after the dog, headed straight for the thick bushes.

"Whoa, wait!" I shouted.

She didn't break stride, and pushed into the bushes as if they weren't even there. Rather than the dense growth slowing her down, the branches seemed to part, allowing her to pass through before closing around her. Was there some kind of pathway that I couldn't see? The hairs went up on the back of my neck. It almost seemed as if Ainsley had followed the animal through some sort of entrance to . . . what?

I had to know.

I sprinted to catch up, then stopped directly in front of the wall of bushes. I took a deep breath and heard a double *caw* coming from behind me. Were the birds watching? And commenting?

Get a grip, Marcus.

I pushed my way into the bushes, struggling to keep moving forward. It was nowhere near as simple as Ainsley had made it look. I had to fight my way through dense brambles that scratched my face and arms, but I kept moving. I must have traveled through five yards of thicket before finally reaching the far side. I stepped out of the bushes . . .

. . . and into a clearing. It was a large space ringed by a circle of huge bushes like the ones I had just come through. The foliage formed a near-perfect circle that reached at least ten feet high, all the way around. The ground inside the circle was covered in rich, dark green grass. Near the center was a pile of massive boulders that stood at least twenty feet high. The rocks were covered in moss, leaves, and vines. It wasn't a natural scene. The rocks looked as though they had been placed there by monster construction equipment. Based on the heavy vegetation that covered the rocks, whatever had made that pile had done so a long time ago.

None of the details about the circle meant anything compared with what I saw next to the pile of rocks. Ainsley stood with her back to me, facing the mound of boulders.

Standing in front of her was a woman—a beautiful woman with long black hair that fell halfway down her back and was so straight it looked as though she had ironed it. She wore a long dress that looked right out of the seventeenth century. At one time it was probably white, but not anymore. The heavy material was dingy and yellowed from dirt and age. The dress had long sleeves with ragged cuffs, and it was covered by an apron that wasn't doing much to keep things clean. The woman stood with her hands on her hips and her feet set boldly apart as she stared at Ainsley with eyes so golden they sparkled.

She stretched her right hand out to Ainsley and said, "Welcome, child. I am overjoyed to finally have you here."

CHAPTER
7

Ainsley stood stock-still, facing the mysterious woman.

I stayed several yards behind Ainsley. I didn't want to stop anything from happening. Whatever it was that was about to go down, I had to believe it would help me understand what this disruption in the story was all about.

"We have waited a very long time for this moment," the woman said with a warm smile.

She seemed pleasant enough, and harmless. Then again, she was dressed in some old-fashioned costume in the middle of the woods. That was freaky at the very least.

"I know you," Ainsley said, as if struggling to dig up a memory. "But I don't."

"You could call me your mother, but you have several mothers. And fathers. We've all been looking forward to this moment."

As the woman spoke, she walked in front of the towering pile of rocks, gently touching the moss-covered boulders. She moved smoothly, as if floating. But she wasn't floating. The dirty hem of her dress and grungy bare feet were proof of that. But it sure added to the general weirdness of what was happening.

"You're not my mother," Ainsley said, though she didn't sound so sure about that.

"I'm not your biological mother, but there is a little bit of all of us in you," the woman replied. "You're starting to feel that, aren't you? Things are changing. Your body is changing. Those changes are allowing our wonderful gifts to flourish within you."

"I don't understand," Ainsley said.

That made two of us.

"You will," the woman replied. "You're a bold young lady. You take control. We sensed that in you such a very long time ago. Even as a baby. It is why you were chosen. And now, once the ascent is complete, you will have tools and strength the likes of which you could never imagine."

The woman raised one hand, extended her arm, and slowly waved it back and forth. Above her, the branches of the trees swayed in unison with her movements. When she stopped, the swaying stopped.

Yeah. Whoa.

"It will be quite remarkable," the woman said.

"This is scaring me," Ainsley said, her voice cracking.

"There is nothing for you to fear," the woman replied soothingly. "Your control will become absolute as you usher in the future. It is the beginning of a wondrous time."

She held her hand out, and a scarlet cardinal flew from the trees and landed in her palm. It was like something out of a Disney princess movie. A really weird Disney princess movie.

"Raise your hand," the woman said.

Ainsley hesitated, then cautiously lifted one arm. The cardinal flew to her and landed on her hand, letting out a series of sharp chirps that sounded as though it was greeting Ainsley. Ainsley looked at the bird in wonder, then suddenly stiffened.

"No," she said, and shook the bird off her hand.

The cardinal flew away and landed on top of a boulder behind the woman.

"If you won't tell me who you are," Ainsley said, "tell me who *I* am."

The woman smiled warmly. "You are who you have always been. Until now."

She reached for the cardinal. The bird didn't move when the woman gently grasped it. But as she brought it forward, the cardinal transformed. Rather than the beautiful red bird, the woman now held a gleaming silver dagger with an eight-inch blade.

I had to hold my breath to keep from gasping in surprise.

"Tomorrow is Samhain. On that highest of holy days, the powers we gave you will fully blossom and create the path that will lead us into our future. Now, give me your hand."

The woman gestured for Ainsley to hold her hand out. The woman's other hand clutched the dagger, as if ready to use it.

Things had suddenly gotten serious. This was no Disney story.

Ainsley took a nervous step backward.

"No . . . no . . . I don't like this."

Whatever spell had been holding Ainsley, it was losing its grip on her.

I couldn't take it anymore.

"That's enough!" I called out.

The woman's expression quickly twisted from warm and welcoming into a grimace of anger.

And she was holding a dagger.

"Cretin!" she snarled viciously as she pointed the dagger at me. "You will not stand in our way again."

Again? What was that supposed to mean?

"Let's go," I said to Ainsley, and grabbed her arm to pull her away.

The woman wasn't going to let us leave that easily. The moment our backs were to her, a huge swarm of white ravens flew out from the bushes in front of us. There was a fluttering chaos of white feathers churning through the air, headed our way.

I instinctively let go of Ainsley and raised my arms to protect my face. We were seconds away from being swarmed by a flock of albino ravens under the control of this strange woman. I backed away quickly with my head down, waiting for the birds' sharp beaks to start pecking at me. Their shrieking war cries pierced straight into my brain as I fell to my knees.

But nothing happened.

The shrieking and fluttering stopped.

I stole a cautious peek over my arms to see the impossible.

A dozen white ravens stood lined up on the ground. Their low, calm coos joined together and sounded like an idling engine. That was cool by me, as long as the engine didn't get thrown into gear. The birds were all looking to my right, intently focused on something.

I glanced in that direction to see Ainsley with her hand held out to them in a *Stop* gesture.

She had prevented the attack.

"Get up, Marcus," she said with surprising calm. "We're leaving."

I cautiously got to my feet, trying not to make any sudden moves that might flip the birds out and send them back into a pecking frenzy.

"Walk back the way we came," Ainsley said. "Slowly."

I skirted around the lineup of freakishly big birds.

Ainsley kept her hand out to hold them back as she rounded the flock from the other side.

The birds stayed focused on her, turning in unison to continue facing her.

The two of us met on the other side of the flock and backed away, toward the wall of bushes.

"Will they come after us?" I whispered to Ainsley.

"I have no idea," she said.

As we were about to hit the bushes, the woman called out, "Now do you see?"

I stole a quick look back to the woman, expecting her to be all sorts of angry. But she stood with her arms folded, smiling proudly. On her shoulder was the cardinal.

"Do you need any more proof of your abilities, Ainsley?" she called.

"We're leaving," Ainsley announced defiantly.

"Go," the woman said with a shrug. "On Samhain you will return."

"Don't bet on it!" I yelled.

The woman's expression turned ugly again. "Do not interfere, cretin," she snarled. "This time we will not show mercy."

This time? What did she mean by that?

I turned and pushed the branches aside to form a path for us to get through.

"Are they coming?" I asked.

"We'll know once we get to the other side," Ainsley answered, breathless.

I fought through the dense tangle with Ainsley right behind me. When we broke out of the far side, we both looked to the sky, expecting to see the flock of vicious birds swooping up and out of the circle to dive-bomb us.

They didn't.

"We're out of here," I said, and grabbed Ainsley's hand.

We ran back to the school, first dodging through the stand of white birch trees, followed by a mad, twisting journey through the pine forest. We made it to the edge of the woods without any problems and jumped out onto the wide stretch of grass that marked the beginning of the school property, and civilization. We stood on the grass, both breathing hard from the desperate run. I had my hands on my hips, looking at the ground, wondering what to say.

"I don't know," Ainsley said.

"You don't know what?"

"I don't know who that was or what any of it meant."

"Let's walk," I said.

We may have been out of the magical forest, but I didn't feel comfortable being anywhere near it, so we headed for the school.

"Why did you follow that dog?" I asked. "It was like you were in some kind of trance."

"I don't know, Marcus," she said with confusion. "I feel like I've just woken up from a bad dream."

"She said you were changing. That your body was changing. Is it?"

"You mean besides suddenly being able to move things with my mind?" Ainsley asked.

"Yeah, I guess. And the bird thing. That was . . . odd."

Ainsley laughed nervously. "Well, yes, if you must know. I'm thirteen. Things happen when girls hit thirteen."

"Really? Like what?" I said dumbly.

She gave me a sour look. It took me a second to realize what she meant.

"Oh."

"Yeah, 'oh,'" she said. "I started getting my period a couple of weeks ago. I can't believe I just shared that with a total stranger. And a boy."

"Get over it," I said dismissively. "So . . . she said those changes are letting their gifts flourish within you."

"Whatever *that* means," Ainsley said.

"Has weird stuff like this happened your whole life?" I asked.

"No! No way. None of this makes sense."

"Do you know that lady?"

Ainsley thought hard and frowned. "I think. I don't know. She looked familiar but . . . I'm so confused."

"When did the accidents start happening? Was it, like, when you started getting your . . . you know?"

She thought a second, then suddenly got all agitated. "No!" she exclaimed. "What does one have to do with the other?"

"I don't know. I'm just guessing here. I have no idea why you can do what you can do, or why that freak can move trees and get birds to attack and turn a cardinal into a dagger. But she sure knows a lot about you. And from what she said, something big's gonna hit the fan tomorrow and you're in the middle of it."

"What is Samhain?" Ainsley asked.

"Halloween. All Hallows' Eve. Big mystical night,

according to people who believe in big mystical things. After what I just saw, I may be one of them."

We got to the school, but instead of going inside, we rounded the building to the front turnout driveway, where parents pulled in to pick up and drop off their kids. School was still going on, so there weren't any cars except for a black SUV that sat idling nearby.

"My mom," Ainsley said. "I almost forgot. She came to pick me up."

"You should tell her what's going on," I said.

Ainsley thought about that for a moment, then said, "No."

"Why not?"

"For one thing, she won't believe me."

I didn't argue with her. I knew the feeling.

"I'm her perfect little overachiever. If I told her I had strange powers and was being asked to join some mystical cult, she'd lock me up."

"Maybe that's not such a bad idea. At least until after Halloween."

"No, I have to find out what this is about. It's actually kind of . . . exciting, don't you think?"

"No, I don't," I said quickly. "This is serious stuff. Dangerous stuff. Whoever that lady and her friends are, I don't see them being good guys."

"Maybe not," Ainsley said. "But I want to know what

they want from me, and maybe learn a little bit more about myself along the way. Who knows? It might be a good thing."

Her one-eighty change in attitude bothered me. She had gone from being confused and scared to actually thinking something positive might come from all this.

"It's not going to be a good thing, Ainsley," I said. "Trust me."

Ainsley gave a cute little shrug and said, "I guess we'll see!"

This was bad.

She started toward her mom's car, then turned back to me.

"Thanks, Marcus. Looks like you may have come here at the exact right time."

"Yeah, funny how that happened," I said.

"See you tomorrow."

Ainsley ran for the car. She seemed way too bright and happy considering what had just happened. She had started out freaked by the idea she might possess strange powers, and now seemed excited about what those powers might be.

It was a very dangerous road to travel.

She got in the car and threw me a quick wave as the SUV turned onto the street and powered away. I was left feeling helpless. I had learned who was responsible for the disruption at Coppell. It was Ainsley. This was her story. But that only raised more questions. Disturbing questions. Questions I had no answers for. I needed help. It was time to get back to Everett and the Library.

As I walked toward the building, the afternoon quiet was suddenly broken by the cawing sound of a flock of crows. My back stiffened. I looked to the sky in time to see a flock high in the sky, flying over the school. They were black birds, so I relaxed.

For about a second and a half. The flock made a quick turn and did a nosedive, headed my way.

"Oh, that's not good," I said to nobody, and took off running.

The birds had appeared black only because they were silhouetted against the bright October sky. They were actually white, and they were after me. With Ainsley gone, there wasn't anybody to stop them. I sprinted for the school, grabbing at my neck for the Paradox key. I yanked the key over my head, and the cord caught on the hood of my sweatshirt.

"No!" I shouted with panic.

I pulled my hoodie off and fumbled for the key. A quick look skyward showed me that the birds were still plunging my way. I was seconds away from being attacked. I separated the key from the hoodie while still running.

The birds were so close I could hear the sharp flapping of their wings.

I held the key out as I ran for the first door I saw, willing the keyhole to appear.

It did. I jammed the key inside, twisted it, and pulled the door open on the Library.

But the key was still in the lock. I had to struggle to get it out. It was a critical three seconds, for it gave one of the demon birds time to attack. It landed on my head and grabbed a beakful of my hair. It felt like my scalp was on fire as the evil bird yanked away, ripping out a chunk of hair. I swept my arm up, knocking the monster off me. I quickly jumped through the door and kicked it closed as a dozen more birds hit it together, desperately thumping against it to get at me.

I stood with my back to the door, rubbing my burning scalp. The gut-clenching reality hit that this disruption was every bit as dangerous as our adventure with the Boggin had been. The only thing I knew for sure was that whatever was actually going on, it was going to come to a head the following night.

Samhain.

Halloween.

The countdown had begun and I didn't have the first idea what to do about it.

CHAPTER
8

THE WHITE RAVENS FLEW into the door, one after the other, slamming into the glass with sickening force in a desperate attempt to get through and attack Marcus. It was futile. Marcus was gone. He wasn't even on the other side of the door. He had returned to the Library. After several violent seconds, the birds flew off as one, headed back over the trees and into the forest from which they had come.

"It's Ainsley," I announced to Everett, breathless, as I ran back to the circulation desk of the Library, rubbing my head where the white raven had yanked out a healthy chunk of hair.

Freaking nasty bird.

The spirit-librarian sat there, calmly reading the red book that had officially become Ainsley's story. There were also several other books stacked in front of him. He'd been doing some research.

"So I see," Everett said, without looking up from his reading. "How's your head?"

"It hurts!" I exclaimed. "How do you think it is?"

One of the remarkable truths about the Library is that the spirit-authors who write the books keep all the stories up to date, instantly. I have no idea how that's possible, but Everett keeps saying how time has no meaning in the Library, so time must have no meaning to the spirit-authors either. Everything that had happened to Ainsley and me in the forest only minutes before was already in the book.

"Her story isn't a unique one," Everett said as he pushed one of the stacks of books across the desk toward me. "I've found stories of other disruptions that took place in that exact same spot."

"At that school?" I asked, surprised.

"Not the school, the town. It's got quite a history dating back to the late 1600s. Apparently it was settled by a small band of people who left eastern Massachusetts to escape persecution."

"What kind of persecution?"

"Ever hear of a town called Salem?"

I thought for a second and the lightbulb went on.

"You mean like where they had those witch trials?"

"One and the same," Everett replied.

"But that was bogus, right? I mean, there weren't any real witches. People were just superstitious. And idiots."

"Aye. There weren't any real witches in Salem because by the time the trials began, they'd all left . . . and settled in Coppell."

My mind raced as more pieces of the puzzle began slipping together.

"The lady in the forest, she made the trees move and the birds attack. And she turned a red cardinal into a dagger. I thought she was going to slice Ainsley with it."

"I guess that tells us what we're dealing with, then, doesn't it?"

"Witchcraft," I said with finality. "That stuff is real?"

"Everything is real," Everett said with a touch of impatience. "Surely you've figured that out by now."

"But that was like hundreds of years ago! You're saying that woman is a descendant of those witches?"

"Could be. Or maybe time has no meaning to witches either," Everett said ominously.

"Wow" was my incredibly lame response. "What about Ainsley? If she's a witch, she doesn't know it."

"But she does seem intrigued by the possibility,"

Everett said, tapping the book. "That's troubling. There's a lot more going on with that girl than meets the eye."

I scanned the books that lay open on the counter with growing dread. They held tales of witchcraft. Real witchcraft. No ruby slippers or flying monkeys here.

"There's something else," I said. "The witch-lady threatened me. She said this time they'd show no mercy and that I wasn't going to stand in her way *again*. What was that supposed to mean? I'd never seen her before! Trust me, I'd remember."

Everett's expression turned dark, as if this news bothered him. He reached out and pulled back the stack of books.

"Go home," he said. "Let me read up on the other disruptions. When you come back, I'll have a better handle on what it might mean."

"You expect me to just go home and go to school and be normal like none of this is happening?" I asked with frustration.

"Aye," Everett replied. "Our work is important here, Marcus, but you can't let the Library take over your life. That would just be another kind of disruption."

I didn't know what to do. I wanted to help Ainsley—that's why I was there. The unfinished story was hers. But I had no clue about how to finish her story. For all I knew, there would be a flock of white ravens waiting to peck me in the head the second I went back to Coppell. I needed help. If Everett could find it in those books, I could wait.

"Want to hear something funny?" I said. "My parents think I'm not doing anything worthwhile with my spare time."

"Can't help you with that one," Everett said. "But you're a smart lad. You'll figure something out."

I headed for the door that would lead me back to real life.

"We're going to crack this, Marcus," Everett called to me. "This story will have an ending."

"Yeah," I said. "Let's hope it's a happy one."

When I opened the door to my bedroom, Lu and Theo were right there, walking away as if we had all gone through at the exact same time. They both stopped and spun around when they heard me.

"Seriously?" Lu exclaimed. "I thought you weren't coming?"

"I wasn't. I mean, I didn't. I went back to Coppell."

"But . . . ," Theo said, pulling on his ear while his brain went into overdrive. "I guess it's true: we always come back at the same moment that we left. Remarkable."

"And a whole lot has happened since I saw you last."

"This is so incredibly strange," Lu said, dumb-founded.

"It's going to get stranger," I said as I passed them, headed for the door. "Let's go to school. Our school."

As we walked (or, in Lu's case, rolled on skates) to good old Stony Brook Middle School—the school that *wasn't* cursed by witches—I filled them in on what I had seen with Ainsley and about the Salem witch connection. They listened without asking questions, which was good, because I didn't have any answers.

Walking along with my friends was so normal. So familiar. So safe.

Until it wasn't.

We were almost at school when the world went wacky. Or at least wackier than normal. My vision went sideways and I lost my balance as if the sidewalk had tipped on end. My ears rang with the wail of a hundred screaming birds. Were they ravens? I took a few wobbly steps forward, stumbled onto the grass, and fell on my butt.

"Run!" I screamed at Lu and Theo.

"Whoa! Why?" Lu called as she and Theo hurried to help me.

I sat in the grass, my head spinning from the incessant screeching of invisible birds. The only thing I could do was bury my head in my arms and hope they'd go away.

"Get down! Cover up!" I shouted. The effort made my head spin even faster. I thought I might puke.

"Are you sick?" Theo asked frantically. "Marcus! What's going on?"

It ended as fast as it had begun. The cawing stopped and the dizziness went away. I cautiously peeked up to see that all was normal. Even my head was clear. It was as if nothing had happened.

"Help me up," I said.

Theo and Lu grabbed my arms and lifted me to my feet.

"What was that all about?" Lu asked nervously.

"I got real dizzy," I said. "Everything started spinning and I couldn't stand up."

"Maybe you have a brain tumor," Theo said.

I gave him a shove. "I don't have a brain tumor. There's nothing wrong with me except . . ."

I couldn't finish the sentence.

"Except what?" Lu asked.

"I heard birds. They sounded exactly like the white ravens that attacked me back at Coppell."

Lu took a quick look around. "Uh . . . no birds here."

"I'm not making it up," I said forcefully. "I heard them. It must be the witch. She's messing with me."

Lu and Theo exchanged worried looks.

"If that's true," Theo said, "it means she can reach right through the Library to get you."

My knees went weak, and not because I was hearing more birds.

"Maybe we should back off this story a little," Lu suggested.

"I wish we could," I said.

The three of us continued to school . . . our normal, everyday old school that I was suddenly liking a lot more than ever before. Getting through the day was tough. I couldn't concentrate on anything my teachers were saying. All I kept thinking about was the world turning sideways and the sound of screaming white ravens. Would it happen again? Would the witch zap me with no warning and drive me out of my mind? It was like being strapped to a time bomb with no way of knowing when it might go off.

It wasn't until last period that the fuse reached the bomb.

Thursdays were run day in PE. Everybody had to run a mile on the track. The faster you did it, the better your grade, which made no sense to me. Gym should be about effort, not talent. But I didn't make the rules, so . . . whatever. Besides, I was fast. Halfway through the mile I was way ahead of everybody else. I think my fear and frustration may have given me a little extra boost. I was rounding the last turn, about to hit the stretch to the finish line, when I heard it.

It was faint, but it was real.

Screeching birds.

The white ravens were back.

I looked around frantically, trying to see where the attack would be coming from. There were no birds in the sky, yet the horrible noise grew louder, as though a huge, noisy flock was closing in on me. A moment later, the world went wonky again. It felt as though I were standing on the deck of a capsizing ship. I had no control and fell to the grass on the infield.

A few guys shot by me, but I didn't care. I closed my eyes to try and stop the spinning, and covered my head with my arms, to protect myself from the swarm of birds.

None came. A few seconds later, the world went right again. The dizziness was gone.

The PE teacher, Mr. Darula, came running up.

"O'Mara? You okay? Did you pass out?"

I sat up and looked around as the other kids sprinted for the finish line.

"I'm okay," I said. "I just got dizzy from running too hard."

I gingerly got to my feet, expecting to feel woozy, but I was totally fine.

"You sure?" Darula asked with concern.

"Yeah, I'm fine," I said, and proved it by jogging to the finish line.

"Fine" was the last thing I was feeling, though. I was one hundred percent certain that the witch from Coppell was reaching out to mess with my head. By the time the school day was over, I had suffered through two weird dizzy spells and phantom bird attacks, but I was no closer to knowing what to do about any of it. There was only one thing I was dead certain about: I was scared.

"We have to get back to the Library and see what Everett found," Lu said as the three of us headed toward my house after school.

I went along with them, but with each step my confidence grew weaker. If the witch was trying to scare me off from messing with her witchy plans . . . mission accomplished.

I didn't want to go back to Coppell Middle School.

I didn't want to face the wrath of some ancient witch.

I didn't want to finish the story, because I was afraid of what the ending might be.

Everett was waiting for us in the Library with a few books open on the circulation desk. He had a mischievous gleam in his eye as if he couldn't wait to share what he'd learned. Theo, Lu, and I pulled up wooden stools like students in class ready to hear a presentation.

"Good news and bad news," Everett began. "Good news is I'm pretty sure I know what's happening at that school, and why. Even better, I know how you can stop it."

"So what's the bad news?" Lu asked.

"If you fail, hundreds of people may die," he said flatly.

I didn't remind him of the extra-bad news that I was cursed by a witch. That would have sounded lame compared with the "hundreds of people may die" thing.

"So who is she?" Theo asked.

"Don't know exactly," Everett said, referring to one of the finished books. "But I found a story that tells the tale of a coven of witches that called themselves the Black Moon Circle. These witches were active near Salem back around 1692. A pretty lofty group of witches, from what I've read. They thought of themselves as far superior to mortals and felt their dark powers should elevate them to a position of authority over humans."

"So they wanted to run the town?" I asked.

"That was the least of it! They planned to create a superrace that would spread their influence far and wide. These witches weren't content to live quiet lives and hide their abilities. Oh no, they wanted control."

"But the people of Salem put them out of business, right?" I asked.

"Sort of. They escaped and fled to western Massachusetts, where they found a quiet little corner of the woods and set up a homestead. It eventually became the town of Coppell."

"Witch town!" Lu exclaimed.

"Do the people who live there know their town was founded by witches?" Theo asked, tugging on his earlobe.

"Doesn't seem so," Everett replied. "But look here."

He pushed forward a stack of four books.

"Completed stories, all having to do with the Black Moon Circle. Seems that every hundred years or so, these witches have tried to pull the same kind of shenanigans they're up to now."

"Which are?" Lu asked.

"They want the world to recognize them as super-beings more powerful than nature itself. Imagine being able to control the weather, the behavior of animals, the wind, even gravity. It's frightening to think anyone could have that kind of power. That's why people have always been afraid of witches."

"You keep saying 'witches,'" I said. "Plural. I only saw one."

"Rest assured," Everett said, "there are others. Witches aren't solitary beings. They draw strength from their covens."

"Swell," I said with full irony.

"So what are they trying to do in Coppell?" Theo asked.

Everett rested his hands on the stack of completed books. "Tomorrow night there will be a black moon on Samhain. It's the fourth new moon of a single season. The convergence of those two events creates a situation ripe for enormous magical power to be used, especially in the hands of a high priestess of a coven."

"So that woman in the woods is a high priestess?" I asked.

"Nope," Everett said gravely. "Not her."

"Then who?"

"It seems to be . . . Ainsley."

"What!" Theo shouted.

"No way," I said. "She's clueless about all this."

Everett picked up one of the books and flipped through it.

"Clueless? Maybe. Capable? That's something else entirely. That coven has attempted this ritual four times before. They find a young girl. A baby. Someone special who is strong and smart but open to their influence. The witches gather the coven and perform an ancient ceremony that takes each of their strongest powers and gives them to the baby."

"And the parents go along with it?" Theo asked, incredulous.

"The parents don't know," Everett replied. "In the past the witches have posed as nannies or performed their spells when they could separate the babies from their families, like at day care."

"That's seriously disturbing," Lu exclaimed. "Evil Mary Poppins."

"The woman said she was Ainsley's mother, and that she had many mothers," I said.

"She may see it that way, but this has nothing to do with Ainsley's natural parents. Ainsley wasn't born a witch; she was chosen. Each time this happens, the coven's powers lie dormant within a baby girl until she reaches puberty. That's when the powers mature, stronger than before, and begin to show themselves."

"That's exactly what happened," I declared. "Ainsley said strange things started happening a couple of weeks ago. The magic was inside her, just waiting for her to grow up."

"And she caused all those accidents with powers she didn't even know she had," Lu said, shaking her head in dismay. "You'd think they'd tell her."

"They just did," I said.

"So what's going to happen tomorrow night?" Theo asked.

"A perfect storm," Everett explained. "The high priestess will channel the power of the coven, through the high priestess, to create a dramatic and horrible display. Blood will be spilled. It's all in the books. In the past, the coven has tried to destroy a dam to flood the town; they summoned lightning strikes to burn the main streets; a plague of locusts descended to destroy the autumn harvest. One time they actually summoned a massive swarm of rats."

"These are some nasty people," Lu said in awe.

"Not people, lass, witches."

"So what's the point?" I asked.

"They're after two things," Everett replied. "The horrible display will announce their existence while summoning the witches of the world. If the covens unite, mankind will be at their mercy."

"It's like the birth of a superrace," Theo said with dismay. "A really unfriendly superrace."

"What's the second thing?" Lu asked.

"Revenge. They hold mankind responsible for forcing them to live in the shadows and hide their true nature."

We all shared nervous looks.

"This may be Ainsley's story," Lu said, "but it's way bigger than that."

"Aye, it is," Everett said, tapping the desk. "Everything I've described is in the books."

"But the witches failed every time," Theo said.

"And that's the good news!" Everett exclaimed. "Each time they tried this dark deed, they were stopped."

"By who?" I asked.

Everett smiled. "Who do you think? By an agent of the Library."

My stomach dropped.

Everyone looked at me. It had come full circle.

"That's why she said I wasn't going to stand in her way *again*," I said.

"Apparently she's onto you, Marcus," Everett said. "She knows you're from the Library."

"She's onto me all right," I said anxiously. "Twice today I was knocked off my feet. It felt like the world was flipping sideways while a flock of freaking invisible birds flew at me. She cursed me, Everett. She wants me out of this story."

Everett scratched his chin thoughtfully.

"Aye. I suppose that's why she took your hair."

"Uh, what?"

"The raven that attacked you. It plucked out some of your hair. She could have used that to put a hex on you."

I wanted to cry. I really did.

"This could pose a problem," Everett said with a frown.

"Problem!" I shouted with frustration. "That's a pretty huge understatement!"

"Let's think positively," Theo said. "How did the other agents stop the witches?"

"They disrupted the disruption," Everett replied eagerly. "It's all about the high priestess. Tomorrow night the coven will gather to unite their powers through her."

"No," I said with certainty. "No way. Ainsley won't do it."

"She may not have a choice, lad," Everett said. "This is a powerful coven. She may resist, but they can charm her as easily as the birds that attacked you."

I thought of how Ainsley had followed that white dog into the woods. She was in some kind of trance and had no control. The situation was looking worse by the second.

"So she's the villain *and* a victim?" Lu asked.

"Aye. Now that she's onto you, you'll have to be all the more careful."

"What am I supposed to do?" I asked with desperation. "I can't fight witchcraft. Especially if I'm cursed."

Everett held up one of the finished books and said, "You must. Find their hollow, the spot where the coven gathers. There will be an altar, which they use to perform their magic. Find it and destroy it. That's what past agents did."

There was a long silence as the impact of this horrifying history settled in.

"What do you suppose the coven is planning to do this time?" Theo asked.

"Hard to say," Everett said. "Based on what they tried in the past, they'll want to make a frighteningly dramatic display. The only thing for certain is that it'll take place on Samhain during the black moon."

"I know where they're gonna strike," Lu said, her voice shaking.

We all looked at her.

"Where?" I asked.

"The Halloween dance tomorrow night. The school will be packed. Ainsley's in charge of the whole thing. That's where she'll be Halloween night, along with hundreds of kids and parents."

Everett looked pained. "You may be onto something, lass. Hurting those children would be just the sort of horrifying demonstration the coven would attempt. Unless, that is, they're stopped."

All eyes went back to me. I suddenly felt cornered.

"I can't," I said. "The witch has my hair. The second I show up, she'll knock me out again."

"Whatever the spell is that's got hold of you," Everett said, "it was most likely cast from the altar in their hollow. Destroy it and you'll be ending her hold over you as well."

I jumped to my feet with nervous energy.

"I can't do that if I'm flat on my back and puking," I argued. "I just can't."

"What about us?" Lu said. "She doesn't have power over Theo and me."

"You don't get it," I said, my voice cracking with nervous tension. "I saw it. That witch controls everything. Trees. Birds. And there was a wolf. I told myself it was a dog, but it wasn't. It was a wolf. We'll never get the chance to find that altar, let alone destroy it."

"Then what about all those kids at the dance?" Theo asked. "This could be a huge disaster."

"And the school is just the beginning," Lu said. "If they pull this off, they may end up coming for you anyway. For all of us."

I was fighting full-on panic. The idea of going back to Coppell and doing battle with evil magic was too much for me to handle.

"Sorry," I said, grabbing my pack. "I'm outta here. I'm exhausted."

"You do need rest," Everett said. "All of you. But I hope you'll be back. If not . . ."

He didn't finish the sentence.

I hurried for the door, with Theo and Lu right behind me.

"They can be stopped," Everett called after us. "History has proven as much."

I pulled open the door that led back to my bedroom and held it for Theo and Lu. Once inside, I pulled the Paradox key out of the keyhole and looped the cord back around my neck.

"I don't blame you for being scared," Lu said. "I am too."

"I'm not scared," Theo said. "I think we can do this."

"Well then, you're an idiot," I said. "You don't have the whammy on you like I do."

"Exactly," Theo said. "That's why I'm not worried. She'll never see us coming."

"Go home," I said, and reopened my door without using the Paradox key. It opened onto my upstairs hallway.

"We'll be back early tomorrow," Theo said. "Before school."

"Yeah, whatever."

"Try to sleep, Marcus," Lu said. "You're just tired."

"I'm just terrified," I said.

The two left without another word.

I closed the door and fell facefirst onto my bed. I hadn't cried since I ran into a pole in kindergarten and chipped a front tooth. Okay, maybe I cried a little during *Toy Story 3*, but that was it. Going up against a centuries-old coven seemed about as impossible as, well, as going up against a centuries-old demon. We defeated the Boggin, but it was close. Now there was another boogeyman to deal with. Multiple boogeymen. It was all so . . . overwhelming. So yeah, I cried.

I wasn't the least bit hungry, so I blew off dinner and told my parents I was going for a run. I said I needed it because school was getting intense. I just didn't say which school I was talking about and what was causing the stress. So I put on sweats and running shoes and hit the road.

It was already dark out, and cold, but running helped me quickly break a sweat. The great thing about running is that it clears my head and helps me think. I've solved many problems while running along the sidewalks of Stony Brook. It's my own little bit of magic that always seems to work. My normal route takes me by my school. I usually do one loop around the football field, then head for home.

When I got to the school, I was surprised to see that it was lit up and busy. There was some kind of event going on. I'd forgotten that it was the night of the fall chorus and band show. I wasn't in either, so no way I was going. I had to slow down as I got closer, because there was a lot of activity. Cars were driving up and parking, and dozens of people converged on foot from every direction, all headed for the auditorium.

I stopped across from the main entrance and watched

as people flooded into the building. There were parents and kids of all ages excited about the concert or performing for their friends and families. I saw nothing but smiles and happy faces.

I, on the other hand, wasn't smiling or happy.

I imagined what it would be like if disaster struck during the concert and the joyous show suddenly became a terror-filled nightmare. I pictured those same people fleeing from the building, running for their lives. How many would make it out? How many would survive, only to be haunted by the horrible memories of those who didn't?

The thought made my stomach twist. I didn't feel much like running anymore, or thinking, so I turned around and headed home.

Back in my room, the only thing that put me out of my misery was sleep. I conked out and didn't wake up until the next morning when there was a knock on my bedroom door. I shot up, fearing the door would be broken down by a flock of white ravens.

"What?" I called out, dazed.

My mother poked her head in. When she saw me, her face fell.

"Did you sleep in your dirty sweats?" she asked.

"My sweats aren't dirty," I said groggily. "They're just . . . sweaty."

"Well, get up. You have company."

Theo and Lu entered the room.

"Dad and I are leaving for work," Mom said. "Don't be late for school. Any of you."

"We won't, Mrs. O'Mara," Lu said politely. "I'll make sure we get to school on time."

"Good," Mom said. "Bye, kids."

She closed the door.

Lu smiled slyly. "Of course, I didn't say *which* school we were going to. Mwahahahaha."

"Where's your head today?" Theo asked me.

I sat on the edge of my bed and ran my hands through my hair, willing myself to wake up and focus.

"I didn't ask for this responsibility," I said. "My father planned for me to get the Paradox key when I was a baby. What if I grew up to be some kind of loser?"

"But you didn't," Lu said.

"At least not so far," Theo added.

Lu gave him a shot in the arm for that.

"Ow!"

"She'll see me coming," I said. "I might be totally worthless."

"That's why you need us," Lu said.

"Does that mean we're going?" Theo asked eagerly.

As much as I tried to deny it and find another way out, I knew there was only one answer. I'd always known. Seeing all those happy people flooding into our school the night before only confirmed it.

I stood up and stretched.

"Did you really think we weren't?" I asked.

"All righty!" Theo exclaimed.

"Just one thing," Lu said to me.

"What's that?"

"I don't care if you wear those sweats, but you gotta use some deodorant."

"Seriously," Theo added.

I couldn't help but laugh. My friends had priorities.

I went into the bathroom, changed into jeans and a T-shirt, put on a clean hoodie, and swiped some deodorant on my pits. I then grabbed the Paradox key, went to my bedroom door, and inserted it into the keyhole.

"You guys sure about this?" I asked.

"I wish we had a choice," Lu said with a rare dose of sincerity. "We don't."

"We really don't," Theo added.

"Then okay," I said as I opened the door and stepped aside for the two of them to go through.

"Happy Halloween."

CHAPTER
9

Everett was standing inside the library door, waiting for us.

He knew I'd be back.

"Feeling better?" he asked.

"Feeling like I hope I'm not making a big mistake," I answered brusquely.

I walked right past him and headed for the far side of the library, with Theo and Lu right behind me. Everett joined the parade that would end at the door that would send us back into the story of Ainsley Murcer . . . and the witches of the Black Moon Circle.

"Anything new show up in the book?" Lu asked.

"Not a word," Everett replied. "I believe this is what you would call the calm before the storm."

"I hope we're not too late," Theo said.

"You won't be," Everett said. "My guess is you'll arrive at Coppell at the same time of day as when you left home."

"I don't understand that," Theo said. "You said time has no meaning here."

"It doesn't," Everett said. "The Library exists whenever the story needs it to. Right now we need to exist on the morning of Samhain."

"How does it know that?" Lu asked.

Everett held up the red book and said, "Because Marcus has the book checked out."

"That's like . . . magic," Lu said.

Everett gave her a wink. "That's the Library."

I reached the far door and stopped, turning to face Everett.

"That's a little too loose for me," I said. "How much time do we have before things get nasty?"

"If Lu is correct, and I believe she is, nothing will happen until the evening festivities."

"When all those kids are together in one place at the dance," Theo said somberly. "What a nightmare."

"Find the altar and destroy it," Everett said. "That'll stop the ascent of the high priestess and break the hex the coven has put on you."

"What about Ainsley?" Lu asked.

"If the power of the coven is taken away, there's a good chance that bond will be severed as well."

"Only 'a good chance'?" Lu asked.

"Witchcraft isn't an exact science, lass. All we can do is stop the disruption and hope for the best."

"So where do we look for this altar?" I asked.

"It must be near the school," Everett said. "That's where all the activity has been centered. Look for a place large enough for the coven to gather but also hidden so an innocent wouldn't accidently stumble upon it."

"The school building is ancient," Theo said. "And huge. It could be hidden in some remote, dark wing that isn't used anymore."

The four of us looked at each other. There was nothing more to add.

"Lots of unfinished books in this library," I said to Everett. "Are they all this dangerous?"

"Not all," Everett said.

"That's a relief," Theo said.

"Just most of 'em," Everett added.

I gave him a sharp look. He shrugged innocently.

I opened the door that led into the boys' bathroom at Coppell Middle School.

"Empty," Theo said. "That's good. I don't know how we'd explain being in the bathroom closet."

"That's the least of our worries," I said. "Let's go hunt us some witches."

I stepped into the bathroom, with Lu and Theo right behind me.

We were back in the story.

"What time is it?" I asked, leading them quickly out of the bathroom.

The corridor was full of kids between classes. The three of us froze for an instant, confused. The school had turned into a twisted fun house. There were hoboes and zombies, princesses and giant cats walking on two legs. And, yes, there were even a few witches with green faces and tall pointed hats.

Lu put it together first.

"It's Halloween," she said. "Trick or treat."

The realization made me relax. Slightly.

"It's eleven-thirty," Theo announced, pointing to a wall clock. "Lunchtime."

"Find Ainsley," I said to Lu. "Stay close to her. If we don't find that altar, it may come down to us keeping her from going to the dance."

"What about me?" Theo asked.

"You and I are going to search the school for that altar. Let's all meet out front at the end of the school day."

"Got it," Lu said, and took off without another word.

141

I looked to Theo and said, "If anything happens to me, you keep searching."

Theo seemed a lot more nervous than he had been the night before. Maybe he was having second thoughts about this adventure. Or third thoughts. Or fourth. Theo was a thinker.

We walked quickly through the sea of costumed kids until we found a set of swinging doors that led to a stairwell.

"All righty," Theo said nervously. "Up or down?"

"Basement," I answered with authority. "We'll start low and work our way up."

Theo took a deep, nervous breath and the two of us started down. When we hit the bottom of the stairs, we were only on the ground floor. We had to hunt for another way to the basement. The corridor was empty, since most of the kids were eating lunch, but there were enough stragglers around that Theo and I didn't stand out. We hurried along, passing the school office, the nurse's station, and, finally, the library. I glanced in through a window to see a bunch of kids hanging out. Like at our school, Coppell's library was a social center.

Kayla was there. I'd almost forgotten about the shy, silent girl. She was at the circulation desk with a book. She dropped it on the counter in front of the librarian . . .

and I nearly screamed. I grabbed Theo's shirt like it was a lifeline to reality.

"What?" he asked with surprise.

My heart raced and my head spun. I pushed Theo back so neither of us could be seen through the library window.

"You getting dizzy again?" he asked.

I opened my mouth but could barely form words.

"It's her," I said. "The librarian."

Theo took a cautious peek through the window.

"What about her?" he asked.

"The witch from the forest."

Theo instantly flung himself backward and pressed himself against the wall next to me.

"You sure?" he asked, his voice rising two octaves.

I risked taking another cautious look.

The woman smiled at Kayla, took her book, and scanned it to check it out. It was all so normal. She looked nothing like a witch but it was definitely her. She wore a plaid skirt and a navy-blue sweater instead of the long, old-fashioned white dress, but I recognized her jet-black hair and golden eyes.

When she finished with Kayla, the librarian waved to another lady behind the counter.

"I'm going to grab some lunch in the cafeteria," she said. "Can I get you anything?"

"Thanks, no, Ms. Tomac," the lady replied.

"Okay, back soon."

Ms. Tomac. That was her name. I wondered if it was made up or if she'd used it since the seventeenth century. She rounded the counter, headed for the door, which was only a few yards away from Theo and me.

"She's coming," I said, and pushed Theo back a few steps.

There was nowhere to hide. If the witch came our way, she'd see me for sure.

Theo stopped at a water fountain.

"Drink," he said, and pushed my head down toward the fountain and blocked me from Tomac's view with his body.

The witch came out of the library, turned the other way, and hurried away from us.

"It's okay," Theo whispered.

I took a chance and straightened up to watch her.

"I thought she was getting lunch," I said. "Cafeteria's the other way."

I moved to follow her, but Theo stopped me.

"Whoa. If she sees you, she'll twist your head around again."

"Yeah, but we gotta see where she's going," I said, and kept moving.

Theo followed reluctantly.

There was nothing remotely witchy about the woman. She looked every bit like a normal person. I began to wonder if I was mistaken.

She reached a fire door at the end of the corridor and blasted through with no hesitation.

"Come on," I said, and we sprinted to catch up.

When we got to the door, I opened it cautiously, fearing she'd be waiting for us on the other side.

"Uh-oh," Theo said.

Beyond the door was a stairwell that led down.

"I guess we found out how to get to the basement," Theo said with dread.

Tomac had already gone down. Without stopping to think, I hurried after her. Theo closed the door gently and caught right up with me. As we descended, the air grew cooler. We were definitely going deep into the bowels of the school. The floor on the next level down was cement, not linoleum. We had hit bottom. There was only one way to go and that was through another set of heavy fire doors. I opened one of the doors cautiously and peeked in.

On the other side was a large room filled with stacks of supplies. There was everything from toilet paper to cleaning fluid to fluorescent lightbulbs. This was where the janitors stored the stuff that kept the school running. It was a labyrinth of cardboard boxes piled to the ceiling.

I took a tentative step forward, but Theo grabbed my shoulder to stop me. He shook his head. Can't say that I blamed him. It was a dark basement, and there was no way to know if a witch lurked around the next turn.

I gently took his hand off my arm and gestured for him to stay put. He shook his head again. I guess being alone freaked him out more than coming with me, so the two of us moved on.

The only light came from old, bare lightbulbs hanging from the ceiling that were spaced so far apart there were more stretches of shadow than patches of light. I listened, hoping to hear footsteps that would tell us how far ahead the witch had gone, but I heard nothing.

Was this a trap? Did she know we were following her the whole time? Was she hiding in the shadows waiting for us to stumble by so she could throw another spell at us?

I walked forward slowly, with Theo right on my tail. Neither of us said anything for fear the witch would hear. Though the basement was cold, I was sweating like it were a sauna. We made a few turns past stacks of boxes. Each time I poked my head around a corner, I feared Tomac would be standing directly in our path.

Theo heard something and pulled on my shirt to stop me. He pointed to his ear as if to say, *Listen*. I heard it too. The sound was faint but distinct. It was a crunching sound, like the kind you make when you crack your knuckles. It kept going, the longest knuckle crack in history. I heard a whimper, as if the knuckle cracker was in pain. Theo and I took the chance and moved closer, creeping around a few more corners. The sound grew steadily louder and more intense. So did the pained whimpers. I had no idea what was happening, but it didn't sound good.

Worse, it sounded gruesome.

I rounded yet another stack of boxes and stopped so suddenly that Theo ran into me from behind. The space ahead widened out into a workshop. There were long tables strewn with wrenches, hammers, saws, and screwdrivers. It was probably where the school's maintenance staff worked. It looked nothing like a witch's altar . . .

. . . but what we saw next to it was definitely straight-up witchlike.

The librarian stood in the center of the space with her back to us. At first I thought she was dancing, because she was moving in a slow rhythm, rolling her shoulders and swiveling her head. But there was no music and it was like no dance I had ever seen. With every movement, loud crunching sounds echoed through the room. It was both fascinating and gross.

Theo's eyes were as big as headlights as we watched

the woman squirm and twist, painfully contorting her body, letting out small sighs with each new pop and crack. It lasted for several seconds before we realized what was happening.

Tomac's body was changing. It started slowly, but once under way, the transformation took only a few seconds. She crouched down near the floor and tucked her chin into her chest. With one last pained gasp, this human-looking witch turned into something completely different. Any hint of human shape was gone. The cracking grew frantic; her body writhed as if small animals were trying to poke out from beneath her skin; her dark clothing faded to white, and in seconds the librarian was gone.

In her place was the white wolf with the black blaze between its eyes.

Theo let out a small whine of shock.

I slapped my hand over his mouth. The last thing we needed was to be trapped in that basement with a vicious wolf-witch.

The beast shook like a dog that had just come out of the water, then scampered off, trotting deeper into the dark basement.

I looked to Theo, my hand still over his mouth. His eyes were comically wide and scared, but his body relaxed. He nodded as if to say, *I'm okay,* so I lowered my hand.

"We gotta follow it," I whispered. "It could lead us to the altar."

Theo looked into the darkness ahead as if debating whether to step into the unknown. He took a deep breath, exhaled, and nodded.

We hurried after the wolf without another word. It was critical for us to be quiet. If the witch had wolf hearing, there was an even greater chance of being discovered. I didn't even want to think about whether or not she could smell us.

Theo and I moved quickly through the workshop and found ourselves walking past large steel tanks with lots of valves and gauges. They had to be the boilers that heated the school. They looked ancient, as if they'd been there for fifty years. The metal tanks cracked and pinged as steam moved through the overhead pipes on the way to the building above.

Running through the basement was like traveling back in time. We moved past the active boilers and found ourselves next to much older tanks that were no longer in use. Brown rust ran along every seam and dust caked the flat surfaces. These things hadn't been used in years. It was probably more trouble to get them out than to leave them to rust.

Theo and I kept moving forward because there was nowhere else for the wolf to have gone. The overhead bulbs grew fewer and farther between, but at least they were still burning. The air grew colder too. I didn't know if that was because we were moving away from the active boilers, or because we were going deeper underground.

The corridor narrowed and the steam pipes ended as we reached a wood-frame doorway. Beyond was darkness.

I stopped. As much as I wanted to find that altar, I wasn't about to walk into the pitch dark after a supernatural wolf.

"This is the end of the foundation," Theo whispered while tugging on his ear.

"Then what's through there?" I asked.

"Maybe the remains of a different structure. This building has been here a long time. They probably built it around whatever was here before."

I poked my head into the dark space, trying to get my eyes to adjust to the dark. It smelled like old, wet wood.

"It's like finding an archaeological site," Theo said.

"Or maybe the perfect place to hide a witch's altar," I added.

I took out my phone. I couldn't get a signal, but the flashlight still worked. I aimed the beam at the floor, keeping the light from shooting too far ahead.

"Let's go find it," I said.

Theo's curiosity was stronger than his fear. He followed me without hesitation through the doorway and even deeper into the past. What we found was a long, dark tunnel with a dirt floor. The walls were no longer cement blocks. Instead, they were made up of thousands of stones perfectly fitted to one another. The low ceiling was made of rotted wooden planks and more stones. It seemed like one sneeze and the whole thing would tumble down on our heads.

"We're nowhere near the school anymore," I whispered.

"This tunnel wasn't part of the original building," Theo whispered back. "Maybe it was built for something else."

"Like what?"

He didn't answer. He didn't have to. We were both thinking the same thing. This tunnel could have been built by the witches when they first settled in Coppell.

We moved forward quickly but cautiously. Since I kept the beam of light on the dirt floor, we couldn't see very far ahead.

"Ahhh!" Theo let out a muffled cry.

"What?" I whispered.

"Something grabbed me," he whispered, frantic.

He was struggling with something I couldn't see. I reached back to grab him, but my hand found something else instead. At first I thought it was a snake and nearly screamed, but I quickly realized the truth and kept calm.

"Roots," I whispered. "From the trees over us."

Roots dangled down like thick strands of hair. I shoved a few out of Theo's way, causing a shower of dirt to rain down on us. We both covered our heads, expecting a cave-in. I held my breath and waited, but nothing else fell.

"Dumb roots," Theo said, brushing the dirt out of his hair. Theo hated being dirty.

"Stay focused," I whispered. "And be quiet!"

We continued on cautiously, holding our hands out to brush aside any other stray roots that might be in our way. My heart was pounding. I didn't want to say it, but I was afraid the next thing we'd touch would be the fur of a wolf.

"Look," Theo whispered, pointing ahead.

The tunnel continued for another thirty yards or so. At the end was a faint, warm glow. I turned off the flashlight and our eyes quickly adjusted enough for us to be able to shuffle forward without it. We must have walked a few hundred yards away from the school. But to where?

We slowed down when we reached another doorway framed by rotted wooden beams. Theo and I exchanged nervous looks. There was no turning back. We cautiously moved forward and poked our heads through the doorframe to see . . .

. . . a huge underground room.

It looked to be the subterranean foundation of an ancient building. The walls were made of the same type of rocks that we had seen in the tunnel. The ceiling was much higher than the tunnel, though it didn't look to be any sturdier. It was at least twelve feet from the dirt floor and looked as if it would crumble if I so much as farted. Daylight filtered down through cracks in the uneven dome, giving the room an eerie glow.

The rotten ceiling planks were shored up by several columns of heavy, dark timber that looked to have been cut from the skeleton of an old ship. At least twenty columns ringed the room. Close to the walls and roughly five yards apart, they ran from floor to ceiling like a rack of ribs.

The ancient vault must have been a couple hundred years old, but what stood in the center of the cavern was much newer. It was a modern wire fence, the kind you see around a school playground. It formed a five-yard-wide circle that stretched nearly to the ceiling. A heavy padlock sealed off a hinged door. The fence was there to keep people out, and away from what was inside.

It was a table.

An old stone table.

An altar.

We'd found the hollow of the Black Moon Circle.

The altar was a large slab of granite, the size of a door, lying flat on top of two large stones. It was solid. Flintstone solid. It must have taken some serious muscle to get it down there. Or some serious witchcraft. The surface was around three feet off the ground and covered with candles of all shapes and sizes. None were lit, but they had been at one time: wax had dripped down from them and hardened on the slab's surface. There were a few ancient-looking books open on top of the altar, as well as some hand tools that I couldn't identify from where Theo and I stood.

I took a step closer, but Theo stopped me and pointed to the far side of the cavernous room.

The white wolf was there, prowling around the outside of the fence.

We backed off and ducked into the tunnel to stay out of sight.

The wolf did a few laps, then padded over to an archway on the opposite side of the cavern. She stood there for a moment, looking into the darkness.

I looked to Theo. *What is she doing?* Theo could only shrug.

The wolf suddenly threw her head back and let out a piercing howl that shook the ancient foundation. It kind of shook my confidence too. It was so sudden and so chilling that I had to cover my ears. It was a long, sustained wail that I feared might rattle the support columns and bring the ceiling crashing down on our heads.

The wolf stopped to take a breath, then wailed again.

I thought I'd go out of my mind. The sharp yowl was ghostly, as if coming from a creature not natural to this life, or any other. It cut through to some dark part of my brain and made me want to howl back. I think I might have, if the wolf hadn't stopped suddenly. The cavern was once again silent. The wolf focused on the archway as if waiting for something.

Another sound grew louder. Something was moving beyond that archway, coming closer.

"I don't want to be here," Theo whispered.

A moment later, there was a flurry of activity at the mouth of the archway. The wolf's howl suddenly made sense. She had sent out a call. A summons. A pack of white wolves flooded into the cavern, bounding over one another, growling and whining.

Theo took a step backward, and I had to force myself not to do the same. I had to see.

The wolves scrambled through the archway like a pack of wild animals. Because they were. I almost expected them to attack one another, snarling and nipping like angry dogs. But when they hit the open space, they fell into an intelligently formed line and circled the fence like they'd practiced the routine. Like perfectly trained dogs, they formed a circle around the fence until every last one had joined. Then, as if on cue, they all sat down facing out.

We had found the rest of the Black Moon Circle.

I had been so focused on the wolves that I hadn't been watching the librarian-witch-wolf. Tomac. While the animal ballet was going on, she had transformed back into human form. Or was it witch form? She was wearing the long white dress I had first seen her in.

The animals sat quietly as Tomac strolled slowly around the circle, looking at each in turn, touching some on the chin and others on the top of the head, greeting them all individually. The animals looked up at her like obedient puppies. Big, scary puppies.

"Welcome home," she announced to the group. Her voice was calm and sweet, as if she were about to read a bedtime story to this freaking pack of wolves.

"It has been such a long time since we were together last. Thirteen years. In some ways the blink of an eye, in others an eternity. We gathered here those many years ago to begin the ritual of the ascent. Tonight, it will be completed."

She walked slowly and deliberately outside the fence

to a smaller stone table tucked up against the wall. It was a miniature version of the altar, complete with candles.

"I know some have doubts," she said to the group. Or the pack. Or the coven. Or whatever the heck they were. "We have attempted this ritual four times and achieved nothing but frustration and failure. I swear to you, this time will be different."

She reached down and picked up what looked like a small doll from the table.

"This time there will be no outside interference. As the black moon ascends, our brothers and sisters will rise to shine our light on a world that has forced us to cower in darkness. Not any longer. When the shadow of the black moon stretches over their spilled blood, we will be avenged."

I glanced at Theo. He looked about as sick as I felt. Everything we feared was true. The books said it. Something horrible was going to happen that night.

"Now, run with me," Tomac commanded. "But return here by sundown, for by night's end the Black Moon Circle will once again run free."

With a quick series of violent cracking sounds, the witch transformed back into the white wolf. As soon as the change was complete, the other wolves jumped up, ready to roll. The Tomac-wolf took off for the archway.

The other wolves howled and barked as they ran after her. They disappeared through the arch in a flurry of fur and fangs, their growls and grunts growing faint as they left the hollow behind.

Theo and I didn't move. I don't know if it was because we were shocked by what we had seen, or because we were afraid one of the wolves might come back. We stood there for a good five minutes before I dared to take a step into the cavern.

"Don't," Theo warned.

I ignored him and walked up to the fence to peer at our target.

The altar.

"This is it," I said. "We have to destroy it."

I now had a better view of the tools on top of the altar. Besides the candles there were various plates and books, along with a nasty-looking dagger with a blade that had to be at least eight inches long. It was the same silver blade that the cardinal had transformed into. I hated to think what it might be used for. Tomac had said something about spilled blood, and the day before, she had looked as though she was going to cut Ainsley. The idea made me want to tear down the barrier with my bare hands. I curled my fingers around the fence's links and shook it. It barely budged. I yanked on the padlock, hoping it was unlocked. It wasn't.

"There's no way we can get in there," I said. "That's why she said there won't be any interference. The altar's totally protected."

"Uh, Marcus," Theo said, his voice shaky. "I don't think that's what she meant." He was standing next to the smaller table, against the wall. "You gotta see this."

On the table were a few more melted candles, a couple of smaller knives, and a crude doll made of cloth. It looked like something a kid might make by stuffing a sock. It was the doll that Tomac had picked up to show the others.

"She said there wouldn't be any outside interference," Theo said. "She wasn't talking about the fence."

"Not following," I said.

Theo picked up the doll and pointed to a tuft of dark hair pinned to the top of what was supposed to be its head.

"Look familiar?" he asked, and held the doll next to my face.

It took a second for me to register what he meant.

But I got it.

"Is that my hair?" I yelled in disgust, and grabbed the doll.

"It's a voodoo doll," Theo said. "This is how she casts those spells on you. You're the one she's preventing from interfering."

"Why is she so worried about me?" I asked, stunned.

"Oh, I don't know," Theo said. "Maybe because you're the only one who knows about Ainsley and what's really going on? And the only reason the witches failed before was because agents from the Library stopped them? Do you think that might have something to do with why she's worried? Hmm?"

He was making way too much sense.

"Yeah, well, she's not gonna mess with me anymore," I said with defiance, and pulled the straight pin out of the doll. With two fingers, I removed the hair and jammed it into my pocket.

"Done," I said. "Now let's figure out how to crush this thing."

We heard a sound coming from the tunnel that led to the school. It was an unmistakable whimper and a short howl.

"Another wolf," Theo gasped.

I looked around frantically, desperate to find a place to hide. There was nothing. We had only one choice.

"This way," I said, running for the archway that the wolves had disappeared through.

"After the wolves?" Theo asked, horrified.

"Or we could face the one that's about to show up," I said.

There was no debate. He ran after me. We sprinted

for the archway as another howl sounded from the tunnel behind us. The wolf was getting closer. I could only hope that it hadn't smelled us.

The archway led to a set of stone stairs. I stumbled on the uneven surface as I quickly climbed, headed for the light above. The stairs were steep. They twisted once, then continued higher and finally led out into the sun.

We climbed out of the dark hole and found ourselves surrounded by a jumble of boulders covered in weeds and vines. If you didn't know what was underground, the hole leading to the stairs would look like nothing more than a narrow opening to a cave. The only hint that it was anything more than that was a rusted DANGER: KEEP OUT sign fixed to one of the boulders. The sign was so old I could barely make out the letters. It wasn't until I climbed up and over the pile of rocks and jumped down to the ground that I realized where we were.

"Oh man," I said, breathless. "This is it."

Theo jumped down next to me, brushing dirt off his nicely ironed shirt.

"What do you mean?" he asked.

"This is where Ainsley and I met Tomac."

The vine-covered rock pile was in the center of a clearing sealed off from the rest of the forest by a ring of thick brambles. The growth was so dense there was no way anybody could accidentally stumble upon the place.

"They've probably had their hollow protected like this for centuries," I added.

"This is bad, Marcus. I don't see how we can destroy that altar."

I stared at the rock pile that stood like a fortress, protecting the hollow of the Black Moon Circle. My mind raced, trying to come up with a plan. Any plan.

I came up empty.

"Look," Theo said, pointing to the sky.

I looked up, not sure what he was pointing to. The sky was clear blue, without a single cloud.

"What?" I asked.

"Don't you see it?"

It took a few more seconds, but once I spotted it, it was all I could see. Looming in the vast blue sea of the sky was a perfect dark circle. It was faint but unmistakable.

"It's the black moon," Theo said in awe.

It hung over us like an ominous hole in the sky, a dark warning of what was to come.

"We've got to stop Ainsley from getting to the dance," I said, barely above a whisper.

CHAPTER

10

Theo and I had to get back to Coppell.

I went straight for the wall of bushes that ringed the sinister coven circle.

"Whoa, you sure about this?" Theo called to me as I was about to dive headfirst into the wall of thick growth.

I didn't stop to answer. With my arms held out in front of me, I leapt into the brambles, pushing aside branches to keep my face from getting slashed. The witches' route in and out of there wasn't clear, but the thicket was no more than five yards deep. We'd be through in no time.

Or so I thought.

The more branches I pushed aside, the thicker they seemed to grow. I had picked the worst spot to charge through, but it was too late to go back. We were half-way out of there.

"There must be a smarter way," Theo whined.

He was right behind me and had to keep ducking to avoid getting hit by the branches that snapped back in my wake. The brush was so thick it was like fighting through a pot of spaghetti. I stopped, caught my breath, and looked around for an easier route.

"I don't remember the way I went yesterday," I said, breathless. "It can't be far. We're probably only a few feet from the other side and—"

The words caught in my throat as I realized the truth. I hadn't made a mistake. This was the exact same spot I had pushed through the day before. But things had changed.

No, they *were* changing, right before my eyes.

The branches directly in front of us were growing fast. Impossibly fast. Vines twisted and spread as leaves and thorns sprang from the new growth. Hundreds of new sprouts appeared as the vines interlaced to create an impenetrable living wall.

I could only watch in wonder as the unnatural show played out before my eyes.

"She knows we're here," I said gravely.

"What?"

A long black vine reached from behind Theo like a

predatory python and wrapped around his waist. Before either of us could react, it tightened and, with a powerful jerk, pulled him back the way we had come.

"Whoa!" Theo screamed in surprise as his feet were lifted off the ground.

He was yanked back so quickly and violently that it took only a second before he disappeared into the thick growth. He was gone in an instant, and the green shrubs closed tight in his wake.

"Theo!" I yelled, and chased after him, pushing through the bushes.

I yanked the twisted growth out of my way, desperate to catch up. I didn't even care about the branches that whipped and whacked into my face. I had to get to Theo before Tomac did.

When I finally burst into the circle, Theo was on the ground looking stunned. The vine that had lassoed him was slipping back into the hedge like a retreating snake.

"You okay?" I asked as I knelt next to him.

"That's a dumb question," Theo replied. "No, I'm not. Did you see what happened?"

"Yes," I said, pulling him to his feet. "We'll find another way out."

"There is no other way out," a woman said calmly.

We both spun around to see Tomac standing next to

the rock pile. Her golden eyes bore into me in a way that I can only describe as hateful.

"You should have heeded my warnings and kept away," she said casually, as if discussing the weather.

"We're not gonna let you hurt any kids tonight," I said boldly.

Tomac shook her head as if fed up with two annoying kids.

"You people from the Library are a tenacious lot."

I shot a look at Theo.

His mouth hung open.

It was true. She knew all about the Library.

"You cretins have obstructed the coven's rightful destiny for centuries. I don't know whom I hate more: you, or the wretched people of Salem who tried to destroy us."

I sure hoped she didn't figure out that I'd taken my hair back from her voodoo sock puppet.

"What happened in Salem was a long time ago," I said. "You can't blame people today for that."

The witch's golden eyes flared angrily. I guess I'd hit a nerve.

"You think the persecution ended in Salem?" she said with bitterness. "Throughout time, humans have tracked us down. Hunted us. You created lies and told melodramatic stories about us. All because of your own

166

ignorance. I have seen it throughout the ages. What you don't understand, you destroy. It's so much easier than trying to learn. You crush our magic so you can continue to live your pitiful human lives in blissful ignorance, thinking you have control over the natural world. Well, you have failed. Miserably. The coven is very much alive, and now we will fight back."

"Just for revenge?" Theo asked.

"For survival," she spat, a mad light growing in her golden eyes. "Once the high priestess ascends and the sacrifice is made, the power of all covens will be unified. The stories of witchcraft you have shared for entertainment will become reality. The human blood that flows tonight will become the lifeblood of the new coven."

The witch half walked, half floated toward us as if being carried on the breeze.

"Marcus?" Theo whispered nervously. "What do we do?"

I wished I had an answer.

Tomac came to within inches of Theo and stared him square in the eye. Theo did his best not to look scared, but he was shivering like a terrified rabbit.

"And what to do with this one?" she asked as she reached up and touched his hair.

"Nothing," I said quickly. "He's just along for the ride. I'm the agent from the Library."

The witch shot a look at me, floated to a spot directly in front of me, and looked me straight in the eye. I had just as much trouble holding her gaze as Theo did, but I tried not to show it. It wasn't easy. Looking into her golden eyes was like staring into a sea of mad magic.

"Such a noble young fellow," she said with a smirk. "What hold does the Library have over you? Do they send ravens to haunt your thoughts?"

"No, that's just you. It kind of sucks, to be honest."

I really, *really* hoped the voodoo doll didn't work anymore.

She took a step closer until our noses were nearly touching.

"If you interfere with the ascent," she said with a fierce intensity that actually made me dizzy, "I will twist your brain inside your skull until you beg for the sweet relief of madness to mask the pain."

This wasn't going well.

"Incoming!" a voice shouted from . . . somewhere.

A small object came sailing up and over the top of the bushes, headed our way. It looked like a roll of red Life Savers, but it trailed smoke. It hit the ground to my left, spewing out sparks.

"Fuse!" Theo shouted.

A second later, the thing exploded with a loud, sharp crack that sounded like a gunshot.

Both the witch and I jumped away in surprise.

"Fire in the hole!" came another shout as two more smoking fuses sailed toward us from somewhere outside the circle.

I had no idea of what was going on and didn't really care because it was an opportunity. I grabbed Theo and pulled him toward the wall of bushes. The second two objects fell behind us and exploded with ear-shattering cracks.

"M-80s!" I shouted as we leapt into the bushes.

A quick look back showed that the witch was gone. I didn't know whether she was running from the incoming barrage or heading for the small altar in the underground cavern to throw some voodoo my way. Either way, it was our chance to get out of there.

As Theo and I pushed our way through the bushes, two more explosions reverberated through the forest.

"Is somebody attacking her?" Theo called out.

"I hope so!" I called back.

This time the bushes didn't grow in front of us. The witch was busy elsewhere. If she was headed underground, it wouldn't be long before she discovered that the voodoo doll was bald. I wanted to be as far from there as possible when that happened.

There was one more explosion, followed by a couple of excited whoops coming from the forest we were pushing toward. We were nearly out of the brambles when I heard a high-pitched gas engine fire up. Finally, we burst out of the bushes and saw who was making all the noise.

A three-wheeled ATV sped away through the pine forest. Driving was Nate Christmas. One of his buddies sat behind him, waving his fist in triumph. Both were whooping and hollering with glee.

We watched them drive away with dirt and pine needles kicking up in their wake.

"They didn't know we were there," Theo said, breathless. "They were just lighting off M-80s."

"Fire in the hole!" Nate yelled.

Another explosion erupted behind the bike. They were still at it.

"Yeah, they have no idea they just saved our butts," I said.

Theo and I took off running through the trees, headed back toward the school. I wanted to surround myself with people. People who *weren't* witches.

"What if she comes after us?" Theo asked.

"I don't think she will. It's too close to showtime."

"What do you think she's going to do?" Theo asked. "I mean, all that talk about sacrifice and revenge and spilled blood, yikes."

"No question she's going to try and hurt people."

170

"It's all about Ainsley," Theo said. "We've got to keep her from going to the dance."

As tired and winded as we were, we didn't stop running until we made it back to Coppell. Classes were still going on, so we found a place near the tennis courts to stay out of sight until the day ended. At 2:05, the bell rang, the front doors flew open, and kids came streaming into the courtyard.

Theo and I ran for the school. When we reached the building, we saw the ATV that Nate and his pal had been riding parked in front.

"Fright Night," Theo said.

"Huh?"

He pointed to the giant orange-and-black banner that hung over the front doors advertising the Halloween dance. "They definitely have that right."

As we pushed through the mass of kids streaming away from the building, we kept scanning the crowd for Lu or Ainsley, but we didn't see either of them by the time we made it to the front doors.

"They could be anywhere," Theo said, frustrated.

"Stay here and keep your eyes open. If they leave the building, it'll be through these doors."

"Where are you going?"

"To look for them inside."

"Hurry. I don't want to be alone."

I left Theo in the rush of kids and continued to search. The thought hit me that I might be able to track Ainsley down if I knew where her last class was. I went to the office to see if I could get that info. It was a long shot, but why not?

The school office wasn't far from the front door. There was exactly nobody working behind the big reception desk. I guess once school was out, the secretary took off even quicker than the students did.

"Hey!" I heard somebody shout.

I froze.

Looking further into the office, I saw Nate Christmas sitting outside the closed door of the assistant principal's office. He was alone. No posse. A short while before, he had been out in the woods setting off M-80s. I wouldn't be surprised if that was the reason he was sitting there looking glum.

I gave him a quick wave and started for the door.

"Murcer won," he said.

That got my attention. I turned around and walked over to him.

"Won what?" I asked.

"She's been blaming me for all the crap that's been going on around here. I guess they finally believed her."

Nate's eyes were red-rimmed, as if he'd been crying. The tough guy wasn't so tough anymore.

"Why? What happened?"

He nodded toward the assistant principal's office. "They gotta blame somebody, and I'm an easy target. I'm not exactly popular around here—I get that. But I didn't do any of those crazy things."

"So tell 'em," I said.

"I did. They think I'm lying. You know why?"

I had a pretty good idea but wasn't about to kick the guy when he was down by saying I knew exactly why. Everybody thought he was a dirtbag.

"Why?" I asked innocently.

"Because it's easier to blame me than to figure out what's really going on."

I couldn't help but think about what Tomac had said about how people destroy what they don't understand because it's easier than trying to learn. She wasn't totally wrong.

"So what's going to happen?" I asked.

"They're gonna toss my butt outta here. My parents are in there now, getting the news." Nate shrugged. "It's happened before. I'm used to it. But this time I really didn't do anything."

He seemed to be holding back tears.

"I know you didn't," I said, and instantly regretted it.

Nate sat up straight. "Then go in there and tell them!"

"I can't," I said. "I don't have proof. But they'll figure it out. As soon as something else happens and you're not around, they'll know."

Unfortunately, that was all too true. More things were going to happen. Bad things. And soon.

Nate deflated.

"They're never going to believe me," he said, totally defeated. "Whatever. Moving on again. New school, new start. It's getting old."

I actually felt sorry for Nate. He was a bully and deserved whatever he got for that, but in that one un-guarded moment, I got the sense that he was a very unhappy guy. If he kept moving around and starting over, putting on the whole tough-guy act may have been his way of coping. It wasn't a good choice, but who was I to judge?

Besides, I could relate.

"I hear you," I said. "I'm not exactly the most popular guy where I come from. I don't like doing things just because I'm told to do them. That makes a lot of people crazy, including my parents. But I'm not gonna change. It is what it is."

Nate looked up at me, and for the first time I saw the person behind the annoying act.

"Yeah, it is what it is," he said. "Kind of sucks."

"You're going to be cleared," I said. "Just ride it out."

Nate scoffed. "Except there are always gonna be Ainsleys out there acting all superior and putting people down. That's never gonna change."

Ainsley.

"Is she in there?" I asked hopefully.

"Nah, she's already done her damage."

He had no idea how wrong he was about that.

I backed toward the exit.

"Just tell them the truth," I said.

Nate shrugged and stared at the floor.

I left the office and stepped into a now-empty corridor. Looking to the front door, I saw Theo frantically waving at me.

Standing next to him were Lu and Ainsley.

Yes!

I sprinted straight for them and skidded to a stop.

"Are you okay?" I asked Ainsley.

"Uh, yeah," she replied innocently. "Why wouldn't I be?"

I looked to Lu, who gave me a helpless shrug.

"Well," I said patiently, "after what happened in the woods yesterday, I thought you might be a little, oh, I don't know, upset."

Ainsley looked me right in the eye, gave me a sweet smile, and said, "I have no idea what you're talking about. What happened in the woods yesterday?"

Theo and I stood there with our mouths hanging open.

Ainsley waited for an answer with a look of genuine confusion.

I shot a questioning look to Lu.

"Ainsley said she hasn't been in those woods since she was a little kid," Lu said.

"Lu tells me you saw something scary out there," Ainsley said. "What was it? Is there anything I can do to help?"

"You don't remember seeing a white wolf?" I asked, stunned.

Ainsley threw her head back and laughed.

"Now I know you're kidding. I am so glad you're going to be coming to school here, Marcus. Your imagination is awesome."

She backed away toward the front door.

"But seriously, if there's anything I can do to help, let me know, okay?"

She walked out the door and down the steps, toward the courtyard.

"But not tonight," she called back over her shoulder. "I've got tons of work to prep for the dance. You're all coming, right?" She pointed to the giant FRIGHT NIGHT banner suspended by long ropes over the doors. "It's going to be a scary good time!"

She hit the bottom of the stairs and hurried off.

The three of us were too stunned to move. We all watched as she bounced happily across the courtyard as if she didn't have a care in the world . . .

. . . and wasn't about to ascend to the throne of high priestess of a coven of murderous, revenge-seeking witches.

"She's either a really good actor or truly has no memory of what happened," Theo said.

"They must have put some kind of spell on her," I said. "How else would they get her to do their dirty work?"

"So what do we do?" Lu asked.

"Exactly what we came here to do," I said. "We ruin their party."

C H A P T E R

11

Theo, Lu, and I watched with curiosity as Ainsley walked casually toward the school's front gate, on the far side of the courtyard, throwing a couple of friendly waves to kids as she passed them. It was like any other day at school for her, except she was at the center of a centuries-old plan to help a coven of witches take revenge against the human race.

You know, *that*.

"We have to stop the dance," Lu said, kicking into Go mode.

"Good, stop it," I said.

"Seriously?" Theo complained. "That's all you've got?"

I wasn't paying attention to them. I was still focused

on Ainsley. What was she doing? What was going through her mind? Where was she headed? I watched as she exited through the wrought iron gate and turned right.

"We need a little more than that, Marcus," Lu said.

I snapped into the moment and said, "I don't know how to stop the dance. Think of something. Anything. Lie. Tell 'em there's a bomb threat, or somebody came down with a deadly virus, or a coven of witches is going to bring down the wrath of nature. I don't care. Just get 'em to cancel it."

I started off but Lu grabbed my arm.

"Whoa, wait, where are you going?"

"You stop the dance," I said. "I'll stop Ainsley."

I bounded down the stairs, hurrying to catch up with her.

There was no way Ainsley was in her right mind. She was just as much a victim as anybody. Maybe she was cursed. Maybe she was being groomed for this night her entire life. Maybe she held the power of a thousand witches wrapped up in one pretty package. But she didn't ask for any of it, and I couldn't believe that if she were thinking straight she'd be going along with it. My hope was that I could get through to that right-thinking part of her brain and derail the Witchy Express.

I ran through the gate and looked in the direction

that Ainsley had gone. When I spotted her, my heart sank.

She wasn't going home. Not unless she lived behind the school. Instead of continuing down the sidewalk or getting into one of the SUVs lined up along the curb, she rounded the corner of the old brick building.

She was headed for the woods.

The woods Theo and I had just escaped from.

"Damn," I muttered to myself, and took off after her.

I poured on the speed and sprinted to the end of the building. When I turned the corner, I saw that Ainsley was moving fast and had at least a hundred-yard lead on me. I didn't stand a chance of catching up with her before she reached the trees.

"Ainsley!" I called.

Either she didn't hear me or she was ignoring me, because she kept walking without a glance back, just like when she had followed the white wolf. All I could do was run after her. I sprinted across the now-empty parking lot, closing in on her quickly, but she would definitely hit the forest before I reached her.

"Ainsley, wait!"

She didn't. Whatever this curse was, it seemed to be controlling her hearing too.

I hit the wide stretch of grass that separated the

parking lot from the woods. As soon as my feet left the pavement, Ainsley stopped. She was about thirty yards ahead of me, on the edge of the forest.

I stopped too. I had to catch my breath.

"Hey!" I shouted, huffing. "Wait up!"

She didn't move. Had she heard me? Slowly, she turned and looked my way.

Yes!

"We gotta talk!" I called out.

Ainsley gave me a sweet smile, a little wave, then turned and disappeared into the woods.

No!

I was about to take off after her again when I sensed something odd. I didn't understand what it was at first, mostly because it made no sense. I simply felt . . . movement. There was nothing specific—it just seemed as though things were shifting all around me. There was a faint rustling that I couldn't place. My fear was that Tomac's voodoo doll still worked and the white ravens were on their way back. But I wasn't dizzy and I didn't hear any screeching birds.

It took a solid ten seconds before I realized what it was.

The grass was growing.

Fast. And all over the place. Thousands of dark green

blades were shooting up at an impossible rate. It was like watching a time-lapse video. I stood frozen, mesmerized by the sight, until I felt a tickling at my ankles.

Hundreds of long blades were wrapping themselves around my feet and quickly tightening. They were coming after me! I tried to move, but the grass gripped me even tighter, keeping me from lifting my feet. My panic grew as adrenaline kicked in, and I pulled one foot up with more force. This time the grass ripped out from the dirt. It may have been hexed, but it was still just grass. It took some strength, but I managed to lift one knee and tear hundreds of blades of grass from the ground. I dropped that foot and did the same with the other. It was a struggle, but I was able to free that one too. But each time I put a foot back down, the grass attacked it again.

I wanted to jump back onto the road, where it was safe, but if I did that I'd never make it across the rapidly growing jungle to get to Ainsley. So I plowed forward, headed for the trees. Each time one of my feet hit the ground, grass lashed around my ankle to try and hold me down. But I was fast. The grabby green tendrils barely had time to reach out and grasp me before my foot was up and out of the way again.

Then the grass changed tactics. It stopped grabbing at my feet. Instead, the blades grew together in front of me to try and trip me. My toe caught on one tightrope-like line, and I stumbled. I cried out in fear. If I fell, the grass would envelop me like a green mummy and pin me to the ground, where I'd never be able to break free. Or worse, I'd suffocate. That image flashed through my head and helped me fight to keep my balance as I staggered forward, pumping my knees and tearing out huge chunks of haunted turf.

Finally, I made it to the edge of the trees and jumped off the lunatic lawn. My feet were safely on dirt, so I turned back to see the grass retreating. Shrinking. De-growing. It took all of ten seconds for the grass to return to its normal length and once again look like a neatly trimmed lawn. The only sign of what had happened were several patches of dirt where I had torn up chunks of sod.

This was no Boggin-like illusion. The witches could control nature. That grass had grown to try and get me. If the Black Moon Circle could do something as dramatic as that, it made me wonder what horrors the coven might be capable of if its plan was carried out and the witches' powers intensified through Ainsley.

She may have been ahead of me and out of sight, but I knew exactly where she was going. I caught my breath and hurried through the trees, headed for the ring of bushes that surrounded the coven's clearing. It killed me to have to go back there, but I didn't know what else to do. I dodged through the grove of tall trees, my feet pounding the ground carpeted with the fallen leaves of autumn and brown pine needles.

Ainsley was nowhere to be seen.

"Ainsley!" I shouted. "Please stop!"

The answer I got wasn't a good one.

All around me, the ground shuddered. It wasn't intense like an earthquake; it was more like the forest floor was coming alive. I heard a crackling sound that grew steadily louder. There was no way to know where it was coming from because it sounded like it was coming from everywhere.

I turned on the speed, desperate to catch up with Ainsley before running into any more attack plants.

I finally saw her through the trees, not too far ahead.

"Ainsley!" I shouted.

My victory was a short one. There was a giant *whoosh* as all around me the forest floor exploded. Thousands upon thousands of fallen leaves flew up into the air and swirled around. I was caught in a tornado of leaves and pine needles that created a near blackout. I couldn't see anything but streaks of brown, yellow, and red. They whipped at my face and hands so violently that I had to cover my head for fear of getting poked in the eyes. The pine needles stung my hands like, well, like needles. I tried to keep moving forward but the assault was too strong. I fell to my knees and curled into a ball with my arms over my head to protect myself from the on-slaught. The debris crunched and crackled as it flew into my hoodie and down my neck. The howl of the demonic wind powering the attack was almost as loud as the crackling of the leaves that whipped everywhere. When I inhaled, I got a throatful of debris that made me gag and cough. I was in the middle of a forest, but claustro-phobia was setting in . . . and panic. I couldn't breathe.

I put one hand on the ground and tried crawling for-ward. At least I think it was forward—I was totally con-fused. My hope was to get to a tree and use it to shield me from the barrage. After a few agonizing seconds, I hit something solid and rough. It had to be the bark of a tree. I pressed my face against it and pulled my hoodie over my head. That combination gave me a little protec-tion and allowed me to take a couple of short, shallow breaths. It wasn't much, but it gave me a few seconds to calm down and plan my next move.

The howling wind suddenly stopped. I felt the gentle flutter of leaves as they fell all around me. The engine that was driving them into the air had been shut off. I took a chance and stole a peek out from my hoodie to see I was surrounded by a storm of falling leaves. It took only a few seconds for them all to land and return the woods to normal.

Normal?

The tree I was leaning against vibrated. It was subtle at first but quickly grew more intense. I pulled away and scrambled back on my hands. There was a *crack*. A loud one. The huge oak tree seemed to shiver. It swayed. There was another *crack,* and the tree began to fall as if a lumberjack had been chopping away at its base. And yes, it fell toward me. There were a few more violent cracks as the ancient tree tore apart near its base . . . and toppled.

I had the smarts to keep looking up at it to try to judge exactly where it would fall. I didn't want to commit to diving one way and landing right in its path. At first it seemed like it was moving in slow motion, but it picked up speed as it got closer to the ground. I felt sure it was aiming for me. I waited until the last possible second and then rolled to my right. The mighty tree barely missed me and hit the ground with such a violent thud that I bounced into the air.

I pulled myself to my feet, dazed and more than a little disoriented. After having been through this forest a couple of times, I thought I'd know exactly how to get back to the coven's circle, but the storm of leaves had twisted me around so bad, I was totally lost.

Crack.

The trees weren't done with me. The huge pine I was standing next to was also about to come down. I backed away quickly, only to hear another crack coming from another tree. There were so many trees so close together that I couldn't tell where the sounds were coming from. Any one of the trees could topple. Or all of them could. It was like standing in a minefield. All I could do was pick a direction and run.

Boom!

A massive pine crashed down directly in my path. I put on the brakes and barely missed being crushed. It was so close that I felt the rush of air as the tree fell. I switched direction only to see another heavy pine swaying and toppling. That sent me in a third direction. I had no idea where I was headed. The only thing that mattered was the few feet in front of me and whether or not a skull-crushing tree would land there.

Another tree fell, followed by a smaller one. There was no way to know which tree would be next. In that moment, I didn't care about Ainsley or the Black Moon Circle or the Library or anything other than getting out of the forest alive.

I leapt over a man-made stone wall that had probably been there since the coven first arrived from Salem, and was faced with a towering pine tree that stood higher than any of the others. I didn't have to hear the cracking to know it was falling my way. I stood with my legs apart, waiting until the last possible second to decide which way to run. The tree picked up speed. It was headed right for me. It took every bit of willpower I had to wait until the last moment. When the tree reached a forty-five-degree angle, I jumped to my left . . .

. . . and came face to face with Ainsley.

"What are you doing, Marcus?" she asked calmly.

Boom!

The tree crashed down behind me, shaking the ground. I must have jumped two feet into the air.

Ainsley had no reaction. She looked at me with a curious expression, as if my being there made no sense to her. Or as if she hadn't noticed the forest was crashing down around us.

"What am I doing?" I yelled. "What are *you* doing?"

I kept looking over my shoulder in case more trees were about to topple.

"You're all sweaty," Ainsley said innocently. "Have you been running?"

"Are you serious?" I exclaimed. "I've been chasing you and dodging falling trees and—"

The look on Ainsley's face told me that she had no idea what I was talking about.

"What are you doing out here, Ainsley?" I asked.

Ainsley got a faraway look in her eyes, as if she had to give the question some serious thought. She frowned and started to speak, but stopped when she couldn't find the words. Her eyes took on a new focus as she looked around at our surroundings with dismay, as if seeing them for the first time.

"I . . . I don't really know," she said, sounding confused.

For that one brief moment, I felt as though I was getting through to her and maybe the spell could be broken.

"It's okay," I said reassuringly. "Everything's cool. Let's go back to the school and we can—"

I heard the birds before I saw them.

A pack of white ravens swooped down and swept over our heads, cawing incessantly. Ainsley saw them too and flinched. This was no voodoo doll hex aimed at me alone. The birds were real. They flew as one, sailing over the tall stretch of brambles only a few yards from us. It was if they had flown that way to draw our attention.

"Oh man," I muttered.

We were standing next to the coven's circle.

A section of bushes quivered and seemed to melt away. The thick foliage separated to create an opening that led into the circle.

Standing inside the ring of foliage, between the

opening in the brush and the pile of boulders that hid the entrance to the witch's hollow, was Tomac.

This time she wasn't alone.

A group of men and women stood behind her, staring at us. Some looked to be as old as my parents; others were gray-haired and at least a generation older than that. There were even a couple of kids who looked no older than Ainsley and me. They wore normal, modern clothes and appeared to be no different from people you might see at the grocery store or the movies. But there was nothing normal about this group.

It was the Black Moon Circle.

"Hello, Ainsley," Tomac said pleasantly. "We've been waiting for you."

"We gotta go," I said to Ainsley, and took her hand to pull her away.

Ainsley yanked her hand back while staring directly at the witch. Whatever small crack I had created to get through to the rational part of her brain had closed up tight.

The witch was back in control.

"I hope I'm ready," Ainsley said to Tomac, sounding dreamy again. "I don't want to disappoint you."

My heart sank. Even though she was under the witch's spell, Ainsley was still Ainsley. She was driven to succeed.

"You could never disappoint us," Tomac said with confidence, and held her hand out. "Come."

Ainsley stepped toward the opening in the bushes as if in a trance.

"Ainsley, don't!" I shouted.

It was a waste of breath. She didn't even glance back to acknowledge I was there. Nothing I could say or do would prevent her from entering the circle and joining the coven, whether she wanted to or not.

The only hope I had left of stopping the witches was to keep the dance from happening.

I took a step away, ready to turn and run for the school.

"No!" Tomac shouted, with more than a little anger.

I stopped.

I guess I could have made a break for it, but I didn't want to risk running another deadly gauntlet of nature that the coven cooked up for me.

"You can't do this!" I shouted at Tomac. "You can't hurt these people because of what happened to you centuries ago!"

"To us it was yesterday," the witch said coldly.

"But it wasn't their fault!"

"The entire human race is at fault," Tomac snapped.

Ainsley moved through the wide opening in the bushes, walked right up to the witch, then turned and stood next to her. Her vacant eyes told me she no longer had a mind of her own. She was completely under the control of the coven.

There was nothing I could do for her. I had to try and save my own skin, so I turned, ready to run and brave whatever the forest would throw at me.

I didn't get far.

Standing in my way were two huge white wolves. Their bright eyes were focused on me, and their teeth were bared threateningly. Both uttered deep, menacing growls.

"You have a choice," Tomac called out. "You can stay and experience the ceremony. It would give me great pleasure to have an agent of the Library bear witness."

"What's the other choice?" I asked.

"Having your throat torn out."

The wolves crept toward me, their heads lowered, stalking.

I backed away from them, moving toward the opening in the bushes and into the circle of the coven. I didn't dare turn around for fear the animals would spring. I backed up a few more steps and found myself inside the circle. The wolves remained outside, raised their heads, and howled. As their haunting cries tore through the forest, the bushes on either side of the opening drew closed. The tendrils reached for one another to form a green wall of thorns that stitched together and sealed off the circle, with me inside.

I had failed. Completely. There was no way I was going to stop the coven from forcing Ainsley to carry out its evil plans. The last hope I had was that Lu and Theo could somehow stop the dance from happening. I wished I had taken the book from the Library so I could find out whether they had succeeded, or failed as miserably as I had.

Somewhere high in the trees I heard the cries of the white ravens.

It sounded like laughter.

CHAPTER

12

Theo McLean and Annabella Lu were on their own.

Their task was to prevent the Halloween dance from happening.

When the school day ended, the children all headed for their homes, emptying the building and leaving Lu and Theo alone.

"Let's go see where the dance is going to be held," Theo said. "It might give us an idea of how to stop it."

The two ran straight for the gym, where they found a group of kids in the process of transforming the space into a Halloween extravaganza. Massive black-and-orange crepe paper spiderwebs hung from the rafters; dozens of plastic jack-o'-lanterns dangled from invisible wires, their leering faces appearing to float overhead; strings of orange twinkle lights were spread near the ceiling to give the illusion of orange stars in a night sky; and tangled white cobwebs adorned the basketball hoops and the scoreboard and most everywhere else the kids could think of. The decorations all played into the fun side of Halloween.

None had anything to do with the actual terror that awaited.

"This'll be easy," Lu said. "When the dance starts, I'll pull the fire alarm. The fire trucks will come and evacuate the place."

"What good will that do?" Theo said. "They'll figure out it's a false alarm and let everybody back in. And what if the witches do their dirty work with everybody outside? No, we have to stop the dance from happening."

"You kids here to help?" a friendly voice called to them.

The popular social studies teacher, Mr. Martin, approached them. He was struggling to hold on to a dozen of the plastic jack-o'-lantern decorations.

"The more the merrier," he added.

"Uh, no," Lu said, her brain racing. "We came to say maybe the dance should be postponed."

"Why?" Martin asked with a frown of curiosity.

Lu had no answer. She shot a desperate look to Theo, hoping he could pick up the pieces.

Theo nearly jumped with surprise. He wasn't expecting to have to come up with something on the spot.

"Uh, yeah," he said, tugging on his ear. "The weather's supposed to be bad tonight. Lots of rain and lightning, real doomsday kind of stuff. It would be safer to have the dance tomorrow."

He looked to Lu for backup.

Lu scowled at him. She wasn't impressed.

Martin chuckled. "I wouldn't worry about that. Everybody will be safe and dry inside. Come on, give me a hand."

He turned to head back toward the stage.

"What about the bomb threat?" Lu blurted out.

Martin stopped as if he had hit an invisible wall. The jovial smile dropped from his face.

"What bomb threat?" he asked with true concern.

"You didn't know?" Lu said, then looked to Theo. "Tell him."

Theo nearly jumped again. He gave Lu a dirty look and tugged harder on his ear.

"Yeah, we thought everybody knew," he said. "There was a post. On Instagram. Somebody wrote

196

the dance was going to be a dangerous place and if people were smart they'd stay away or risk being in the middle of an explosion."

"Somebody wrote that on Instagram?" Martin asked, incredulous.

"Yeah," Lu said. "They probably deleted it by now, but still, that's pretty scary. You gotta call off the dance until the police can figure out if it was real or some dumb hoax."

"You saw the post?" Martin asked.

"Yeah," Lu said.

"No," Theo said simultaneously.

Martin put the jack-o'-lanterns down on the gym floor.

"If it was on Instagram, what was the picture of?" Martin asked, staring right at Lu.

Theo gave Lu a smug smile. It was her turn to scramble.

"It was a . . . a . . . skull! Yeah. A real creepy, evil smiley thing. Very scary. Ominous, you might say."

"Show me," Martin said, his concern growing by the second.

Lu took out her phone and scrolled through her Instagram pictures.

"I told you, it's gone," she said. "It may just be a dumb prank, but can we take that chance?"

Martin held out his hand and Lu gave him her phone. He scrolled quickly through her Instagram pictures but found nothing.

"You're right, we can't risk it," Martin finally said, still holding Lu's phone.

"Really?" Lu said with surprise.

Martin turned to the kids in the gym and called out, "Keep working, everybody. I'll be back in a couple of minutes."

He looked to Theo and Lu and quietly added, "Don't want to cause a panic. Let's go."

He blew right by the two, headed for the exit.

Theo and Lu gave each other surprised looks as if they couldn't believe how well their impromptu plan was working, and followed obediently.

"Where are we going?" Lu asked.

"We've got to take this to Mr. Jackson, the principal," Martin replied. "Only he can make the final decision, but I'm going to recommend that he cancel the dance and call the police to start an investigation." He glanced to Theo and said, "Can I see your cell phone? Maybe the post is cached there."

"I don't have one," Theo replied.

"Doesn't matter," Martin said, all business. "Even if the post is gone, I think Mr. Jackson has to call the dance off."

Theo and Lu exchanged excited looks. Theo held up one hand for a high five, but Lu left him hanging.

"Uh, do we really have to go with you to the principal?" Lu asked. "I mean, all he has to do is hear it from you."

"Oh no," Martin replied. "You guys saw it, so you have to report it. Let's hope this is all a prank, but if not, you could be heroes."

"We don't want to be heroes," Theo said. "We just don't want anybody to get hurt."

"Then we're all on the same page. This way."

Martin led Theo and Lu up a flight of stairs and down another corridor of the empty classrooms.

"Do you really think the principal will call off the dance?" Lu asked.

"I don't see how he can't," Martin replied. "He'll have to send out a mass email to all the parents. It'll be a mess, but better safe than sorry."

They reached a door at the end of the corridor. Martin held it open and gestured for Theo and Lu to step inside. They walked past him and into the room to discover . . .

. . . it wasn't the principal's office. Or anybody's office. It was an empty classroom being used for storage. There were a bunch of old desks stacked against the walls, and boxes of used books and several old-fashioned blackboards leaning against a wall.

Lu and Theo stood, staring with confusion.

"This is the principal's office?" Lu asked as they both turned back to Martin, who stood in the doorway.

"Don't bother screaming for help," Martin said with a smile. "There won't be anybody close enough to hear you until Monday morning. Come to think of it, after tonight nobody may come back here ever again."

"But . . . what?" Lu asked, totally baffled.

"You were right about the dance tonight," Martin said. "A bomb is going to go off. Just not the kind you made up."

The truth hit them like a cold, sharp gust of wind.

"You're a witch," Theo said with a gasp. "But you're a teacher. Kids like you."

"Crazy, right?" Martin scoffed. "I'm so incredibly sick of pretending to care about you brats. Tonight it ends. Or begins, depending on how you look at it."

As he turned to leave, he held up Lu's cell phone and said, "I'll hold on to this."

"You're all just evil!" Lu yelled at the witch.

"Not really," Martin said as he backed out of the door. "You should thank me for locking you up here.

It'll be the safest place in the whole school. Happy Halloween."

"No!" Lu yelled, and ran for the door as Martin slammed it shut.

She tried to open the door, but it was locked.

"How is this possible?" she screamed with frustration. "You can't lock somebody into a classroom! It doesn't work that way!"

Theo tried the door as well. He put his shoulder against it and pushed, but the door wouldn't budge.

"I guess maybe it does," he said, defeated. "We're stuck."

Lu glanced out the window to see the black moon near the top of the trees. A razor-thin silver crescent appeared at its edge, like a taunting smile. The moon would soon dip out of sight, along with the sun, on the opposite horizon, turning the world over to the dark night of Samhain.

"It's getting late," Lu said. "I sure hope Marcus got to Ainsley."

CHAPTER
13

I sure hoped Lu and Theo were able to stop that dance.

I was trapped, tied by coarse ropes around my wrists to one of the ancient vertical wooden columns that held up the ceiling of the coven's underground hangout, a perfect spot to witness the supernatural disaster that was gearing up.

The gate of the steel fence that protected the witch's altar was swung wide open. A dozen witches formed a circle within it, surrounding the stone table. A single candle burned at its center, casting a warm glow that spread throughout the ancient hollow. The light danced over the faces of the witches, who stood shoulder to shoulder, staring into the flame. The rest of the cavern was thrown into shadow. I was in shadow. Alone on the outside.

Helpless.

The witches didn't wear robes or tall hats or any other typical witchlike gear. They looked like regular people, which was more chilling than if they were gnarly green demons. It meant that they had been living among humans, undetected, while secretly plotting revenge against them for centuries. How many more of them existed in other parts of the world? If they pulled off this horror show, that question might get answered.

There was nothing good about any of this.

The witches appeared to be in a group trance as they stared unblinking into the single flame while quietly chanting something I couldn't understand.

Standing next to the altar, inside the circle of witches, was Ainsley. She had her eyes closed, and there was a smile on her face as she swayed to the hypnotic chant. This wasn't the girl I had come to know. Ainsley was a razor-sharp perfectionist who did her best to be in control at all times. She was full of life and energy. Whatever hex these witches had put on her had to be pretty strong to change her so much.

Tomac glided slowly around the circle of witches. She held the silver dagger I'd seen on the altar and was waving it back and forth as if cutting circles in the air. That weapon sure seemed like a pretty important part of the ritual.

"Over three hundred years," Tomac announced with icy glee, "we have been patient. There have been failures, but we never lost hope. Tonight, guided by the black moon on Samhain, our destiny will be fulfilled and a new future begun."

The chanting continued, a low, ominous chorus. The witches were saying words that made no sense to me. Was it Latin? Old English? Or some freaky witch-speak?

"We have each given a piece of ourselves to this princess," Tomac said. "Our gifts have lain dormant as she grew, incubating the already formidable magic of the coven."

Incubating? Were they using Ainsley as some kind of vessel to grow their powers?

"When the ascension is complete, she will return our gifts to us, a hundred times more powerful. We will become the axis around which the covens of the world will unite."

The chanting grew louder, more insistent. How did they know to do that? Was this rehearsed?

"Tonight is our rebirth. We will be feared and we will be followed. We will rise and be avenged. The reign of the high priestess will be brief but momentous. Her sacrifice will be remembered by all those who follow, her name forever spoken with reverence."

Whoa, what? Her sacrifice? They might be promoting Ainsley to high priestess but it was going to be a short reign. Whatever they were planning to pull off at the dance, Ainsley was going to be in the middle of it, and she wouldn't be walking away.

I pulled at the ropes that dug into my wrists, desperately trying to free myself. Ainsley's story was about to come to a close. The book would be finished, and it wasn't going to be a happy ending, for anybody.

DARKNESS COMES EARLY IN western Massachusetts. Theo and Lu hadn't been trapped in the classroom for long before the sun dipped below the horizon, along with the black moon, and the world went dark.

"It's gonna be okay," Lu said as she tried to open the locked door for the hundredth time. "Marcus is going to stop Ainsley from doing whatever it is they want her to do. Right?"

She sounded as though she was trying to convince herself and wasn't doing a very good job.

"I wouldn't count on that," Theo replied. "I've seen what that witch Tomac is capable of."

"So then we've got to get of here!" Lu exclaimed with frustration.

She hurried over to the window that looked over the back of the school and the forest beyond it.

"I wish I knew what was happening out there," she said.

She pressed her hands against the wood frame of the window. It was an antique that hadn't been replaced in decades. Lu studied it, running her hands along the frame's peeling paint and then rapping on the glass once, twice, as if knocking on a door.

She smiled.

"Is this like the window that fell out and nearly hit Kayla?"

"Probably," Theo said.

Lu ran her hand along the edges where the glass met the frame.

"This isn't made of thick glass like modern windows are," she said.

Theo went to the window and examined it.

"You're right, it's not a double-paned safety window. You think we can break it?"

Lu took a few steps back, still staring at the window, deep in thought. Without warning, she grabbed an old wooden chair, reared back, and launched it at the window.

"Whoa!" Theo yelled as he ducked.

CRASH! The chair shattered the glass and continued going as if the windowpane had never been there.

"Yeah, I think we can break it," Lu said.

"I hope nobody's down there," Theo said.

The two peered through the empty frame.

The chair had landed on the pavement three stories below.

"Now what?" Theo asked.

Scanning the redbrick facade, Lu spotted a narrow cement ledge that ran the length of the building just below the windows. Twenty yards away, on the same level, was a balcony.

"Now we walk along the ledge to that balcony," Lu replied. "Easy."

"Seriously?" Theo exclaimed. "It's only ten inches wide! If we fall, we're dead!"

"We won't fall," Lu said with confidence. "It's just scary because we're up so high. If it were on the ground, we wouldn't think twice."

"But it's not on the ground."

Lu leaned out to scan the ledge. She looked down at the ground and the broken chair that sat on a pile of shattered glass, and swallowed hard.

"All right, it's scary, but it's not like we have another choice."

Theo looked down at the ledge, wiped the sweat from his forehead, and took a deep, nervous breath.

"All right, I'll do it," he said, his voice shaking.

"We'll both do it," Lu shot back.

"No. There's no reason for us both to risk it. I'll get to the balcony, then come inside and unlock the door."

"Forget it, I'm going," Lu said. "This was my idea."

She started to climb out the window, but Theo held her back.

"I can do this," he said with confidence. "Besides, if anything happens to you, I don't think I can deal with these witches on my own."

"You sure?" Lu asked.

Theo's answer was to stick his head out the window and look to the pavement below. Far below.

"Falling would really hurt," he said, his confidence wavering.

"Then I'll go," Lu said.

Theo ignored her, sat on the window frame, and spun around until his legs were outside, his heels resting on the narrow cement ledge.

"Face the wall," Lu said. "Don't look down."

Theo nodded in agreement and took one more deep breath.

"All righty," he said in a shaky voice.

He grabbed the window frame in a death grip, lowered his head, and ducked outside. He was instantly hit with the chill of the October night, and a wave of paralyzing fear. While keeping at least one hand firmly gripping the frame, he twisted his body so he was facing the building.

"My whole foot fits on the ledge," he said. "That's good, right?"

"It's perfect. All you have to do is shuffle along."

"Yeah. Got it. Piece of cake."

"Great, go for it!"

Theo didn't move.

"You okay?" Lu asked.

"No."

"Then come back in."

"Uh-uh. I got this."

Theo slid his left foot along the ledge, widening his stance. He then slid his right foot, to close the gap.

"There you go!" Lu said encouragingly.

"Yeah, it's easy as long as I'm holding on to the window frame."

"Can you dig your fingers in around the bricks? Like a rock climber?"

Theo cautiously put one open palm on the brick wall to the left of the window. When his arm was nearly straight, he felt for the mortar gap between bricks, then curled his fingers around the top of a single brick. He tested the purchase by pulling down.

"It's not much leverage," he said. "But it's better than nothing."

"Excellent. Take your time. But hurry."

Theo shot Lu an annoyed look.

"Sorry," Lu said with a shrug. "Take all the time you need."

Theo took a few nervous breaths, then slid his trailing hand away from the window frame and gripped the top of another brick. He was standing on the ledge, with nothing to keep him from falling but his balance and a tenuous fingertip grip on the quarter inch of space between bricks. He slid his left foot out, moved cautiously to his left, and brought his right foot next to his left.

"I can do this," he said, his confidence rising.

"I know you can," Lu said. She looked down at the shattered chair and swallowed hard.

Theo moved along slowly but steadily. He got into a rhythm: left foot, left hand, right foot, right hand. He moved only one foot or hand at a time and didn't look down. Mostly he stayed focused on the brick wall inches from his nose, only occasionally glancing to his left to see how close he was to the balcony, which suddenly seemed very far away.

Lu didn't say another word. She didn't want to break his concentration.

It may have been only a few hours until November, with a Halloween chill in the air, but Theo was sweating hard. Salty drops rolled off his forehead and into his eyes, which he didn't dare wipe away. He wanted to stay in contact with the wall at all times.

There were no other windows along the way, just an expanse of brick. It was the balcony or nothing. After a solid five minutes, he chanced a look at his goal and saw that he was only a few yards away. That gave him a surge of confidence. He was going to make it.

"Almost there!" he called out.

He took one more step, shifted his weight to the left foot, and . . . the ancient ledge crumbled.

Lu screamed.

Theo's left foot dangled in the air, but his grip on the bricks was enough to keep him from falling. He pressed his body so close to the wall that he could feel his heart pounding against the bricks.

"Stop, okay?" Lu screamed. "Come back!"

Theo looked down at the ledge. A two-foot-long section was gone.

"I can't," he said. "It's too far."

"But what if the next section crumbles?" Lu yelled.

"I . . . I don't know," Theo called back.

"Don't take the chance," Lu called. "Just slide back and . . ."

Theo lifted his left foot, stretched it over the gap, and rested it on the far side. He tested the ledge as best he could, gingerly putting some weight on it. It held. He quickly slid his foot out even farther, straddling the gap, to allow room for his right foot.

"All righty," he said.

He held his breath, shifted all his weight to his left leg, and . . .

CRACK!

The cement crumbled.

There was no time to think. Theo dug his fingers into the gap above the bricks, pushed off with his right foot, and launched himself sideways at the balcony. The ledge dissolved beneath him, but he was already airborne. Body twisting, he desperately reached out with both hands . . .

. . . to grab on to the white rail that ringed the balcony. Both his feet dangled, with nothing to step onto. He didn't hang there for long, though. Using the strength that came from equal parts adrenaline and fear, he pulled himself up and swung over the railing to safety.

"Yes!" Lu screamed in victory and total relief.

Theo fell to the balcony floor and lay on his back, breathing hard.

"You okay?" Lu called out.

"No! I'm having a heart attack!"

"Seriously?"

Theo took a deep breath to control his breathing, and sat up.

"No, not seriously."

"Well, I am. You scared me half to death."

"Yeah, and I almost fell all the way to my death. You get no sympathy."

Theo stood. Double doors led from the balcony to the school. He went to them and grabbed the doorknob.

"Please be unlocked," he said to nobody.

He twisted the knob and the door opened.

"Yes!"

Without hesitation, he ran inside and sped down the corridor to the classroom where Lu was trapped. When he reached the door, he saw how Martin had been able to lock them inside. A metal bar ran from the lock down to the floor, where it was jammed into a corner. Theo pulled the bar free with one tug.

The door instantly flew open and Lu jumped out.

She threw herself at Theo and wrapped her arms around him.

"That was the most awesome thing I have ever seen," she said. "I'll never call you a wimp again. At least not today."

Theo stood awkwardly as if he had never been hugged by a girl before. At least not by one who wasn't his mother. After a few seconds he relaxed and hugged Lu back.

"That was really scary," he said.

"All the more reason that I'm impressed," Lu said. She pulled away from him. "Now, let's stop this party."

CHAPTER

14

Tomac moved behind Ainsley and ran the tip of the mysterious silver dagger across her cheek.

I cringed, fearing she'd draw blood. Or worse.

Ainsley just smiled. She wasn't scared at all. She had no idea that she was in serious trouble. I'm not sure she had any idea about anything.

"Our powers have grown strong within you," Tomac said. "I know you can sense it."

"I can," Ainsley said dreamily.

"Until now it has been like trying to harness a wild storm. Your emotions were as uncontrollable as the maturing magic. But with the influence of Samhain's black moon, you will finally seize control."

Tomac took Ainsley's hand and lifted it until her bare arm was stretched between them.

The whole time, I had been yanking on the rope that tied my wrists together and looped around the vertical wooden column. I don't know why. It wasn't like it was going to break. But when Tomac took Ainsley's arm and raised that dagger, I panicked and yanked even harder.

This time something happened.

The rope didn't snap, but as I pulled it, the bottom of the wooden column moved ever so slightly. The wood was rotten. Who knows what century this thing had been built, but it sure wasn't as solid as it once had been. The base, which sat on the rock floor, was soft from rot. I pulled frantically, using the rope as a saw, sending chunks of rotten wood and sawdust flying.

Nobody was watching me. All eyes were on the main event, Tomac and Ainsley.

The chanting grew louder. This time Tomac joined in.

"Araba . . . sinquentus . . . dehmino . . . saet . . ."

Whatever *that* meant.

Tomac raised the dagger.

I stopped sawing and watched. I didn't want to, but I had to.

With one quick, slicing movement, Tomac made a cut on Ainsley's forearm.

As much as I wanted to scream and turn away, I forced myself to watch.

Ainsley didn't react. It was as if she hadn't even felt the blade cutting her skin. She kept her eyes on the candle on the altar, still smiling that same loopy smile.

Tomac took a small metal plate from the altar and held it under Ainsley's wound to catch a few drops of her blood. The whole time she kept up the creepy, hypnotic chant.

"Araba . . . sinquentus . . . dehmino . . . saet . . ."

Tomac let go of Ainsley's arm and walked behind the table, where she placed the metal plate down and grabbed the candle.

The chanting grew louder and more urgent. It was like the witches were urging Tomac on to do . . . what?

Ainsley stood there with her hand on her arm to stop the bleeding. She wasn't in pain. She wasn't chanting either. I guess she missed the rehearsals.

Tomac tilted the candle, letting wax fall onto the plate that held Ainsley's blood.

"Our past will become our future," she declared. "Once the ascension is complete, the sacrifice will allow our brothers and sisters to join us across the great void of time."

The witches continued to chant, the intensity

growing. It seemed like a bunch of mumbo jumbo that was just for show . . .

. . . until the show became very real.

One by one, the other candles on the table flamed to life. Their light joined with that of the single candle to create an intense glow that held the altar in a cocoon of warm light. All eyes were fixed on the spectacle, including mine. Within seconds every last candle was burning. It was an impressive trick, and it was only the beginning.

The flame from the first candle grew, creating an impossibly bright aura the size of a grapefruit. As if it had a life of its own, the aura lifted up and away from the wick, leaving the candle's flame still burning. I watched in openmouthed wonder as the same thing happened with each of the other candles. A brilliant ball of light lifted up from each flame and rose slowly into the air like a glowing bubble.

The witches continued to chant and stare at the mass of glowing, floating orbs that lit the cavern up like daytime. Now that it was so much brighter, I saw the look of total joy on their faces, as if the amazing moment they had been waiting centuries for had finally arrived.

Ainsley was watching too, with a smile of wonder and delight.

The glowing orbs continued to rise, growing closer

to the cavern's ceiling. I wondered what would happen when they hit the stone-and-timber roof. Would they pop like soap bubbles? Or shatter like glass? The orbs cleared the top of the fence and got to within a foot of the ceiling, when suddenly, as if on cue, they all flew in different directions. The orbs shot through the cavern in random patterns, swooping and darting around like crazed fireflies.

Some flew right past me, forcing me to hide my head behind the rotten column I was tied to.

The rotten column. Right.

I got on my knees for better leverage and started back in on using the rope like a saw to dig away at the column's base. My hope was that the wood at the bottom was weak enough for me to break the rope through beneath it.

As I worked, I kept watching the light show. When one of the orbs flew past me, I got a closer look at it . . . and wanted to scream. It wasn't just a glowing ball of light. There was a human face floating inside it. I got only a quick glimpse because the orb was moving so fast, but there was no mistake. I focused on the others as they zipped by, and saw the same thing. There was a disembodied head in each one of them.

This wasn't some pyrotechnic display for show. These lights were spirits . . . spirits of brother and sister witches who were being summoned for the big event. Whatever dark power this coven was growing in Ainsley, it was strong enough to bring out even more magic from their past. Just as Tomac had said, generations of witches were returning to this place to take part in the ceremony.

And the sacrifice.

THEO AND LU RAN down the stairs from the upper floor of the school and blasted out of the building into the autumn night.

"The gym," Lu declared, and the two sprinted for the gymnasium entrance.

When they rounded the corner of the school, they skidded to a stop, confronted with a grim reality.

A long line of cars stretched from directly in front of the gym, all the way through the parking lot and out to the road. Each car stopped in turn to drop off a group of excited kids wearing Halloween costumes. The entrance to the gym was lit with strings of orange twinkle lights to form an archway, which the kids ran through to enter the party. Thumping music could be heard from within, beckoning everyone to enter and join in the spooky fun.

"We're too late," Theo said in defeat.

"Not yet!" Lu exclaimed.

The two ran toward the entrance. The moment they passed through the doors, though, they found themselves blocked from the gym by a table set up in the lobby to collect tickets.

A sour-looking adult, the secretary who worked in the school office, sat behind the table. Her only nod to Halloween was that she now wore a black jogging outfit along with a huge Cat in the Hat hat. She eyed Lu and Theo up and down suspiciously.

"Are you Coppell students?"

"Uh, yes," Lu said, thinking fast. "I mean, no, not yet. I'm new. We're both new."

"This function is for registered students only," the secretary said with a snarl.

"But we were invited," Theo complained. "By Ainsley Murcer. She put this whole thing together."

The secretary looked at the two girls sitting next to her wearing THING ONE and THING TWO T-shirts. They both shrugged.

"Go find Ainsley," the secretary said.

Thing One jumped up and ran through the set of doors leading into the gym.

The secretary gave Lu and Theo a fake smile and said, "It's a Halloween dance. Where are your costumes?"

Lu shifted anxiously from one foot to the other.

"Uh . . ." was all she managed to get out.

"We're wearing our costumes," Theo said haughtily. "I'm going as a preppy from Connecticut."

He pulled on his bow tie with both hands as if to tighten it.

"What about her?" the secretary asked, suspicious.

"I'm, uh, I'm a roller-derby girl. But I figured you wouldn't let me in with skates, so this is all I've got. Grrr . . ." Lu gritted her teeth, flexed, and made an angry face.

"Cool," Thing Two said.

The secretary rolled her eyes and said, "Whatever. Wait over there."

She motioned for Theo and Lu to get out of the way, then turned her attention to the next kids in line waiting to buy tickets.

Lu and Theo moved away from the flow of activity and huddled in the far corner of the lobby.

"That girl's not going to find Ainsley in there," Theo said. "And if she does, we're too late."

"There has to be another way to get in," Lu said. "Let's go outside and look for another entrance."

Lu took off running for the front doors. Theo started to follow, when he saw something that made him stop short.

Kayla had arrived at the dance.

She looked absolutely beautiful dressed in a princess costume complete with flowing gown and faux diamond tiara. Her long auburn hair fell in curls to her shoulders, making her look all the more princess-like as she stepped through the festive arbor of orange lights.

Theo stood, stunned. She looked nothing like the shy girl who couldn't speak. She was absolutely radiant. He steeled himself and approached her.

"Hi," he said. "Remember me?"

Kayla smiled and nodded.

"I didn't think I'd see you here. I mean, I didn't think you'd like going to a dance. I mean, you look beautiful."

Kayla blushed with embarrassment and gave him a big smile.

"I hope you have a great time and . . . wait."

Reality had returned.

"You can't go in there," Theo commanded.

Kayla's smile dropped as she looked at Theo questioningly.

Theo took her by the arm and led her away from the rush of kids piling into the lobby from outside.

"There's going to be trouble," Theo said quickly. "It might be dangerous."

Kayla shook her head and frowned, not under-standing.

"Oh man, I can't explain it. But we're trying to stop the dance to keep everybody safe."

Lu ran back into the lobby.

"I thought you were following me," she said to Theo, annoyed.

"I'm trying to keep Kayla from going in there."

Lu focused on Kayla, thought fast, and said, "No, she's gotta go inside!"

"But—" Theo said.

Lu got right in Kayla's face and said, "Can we go in as your guests?"

Kayla looked back and forth between Lu and Theo, totally confused.

"No!" Theo said.

"Theo, we've got to get in there!" Lu said.

Theo was torn, but he nodded. He understood.

"Can you please bring us in?" Theo asked Kayla. "We're trying to stop the trouble from happening. But you have to leave right after."

"Please," Lu added.

Kayla nodded.

"Great!" Lu said.

She grabbed Kayla's hand and hurried her up to the woman in the cat hat.

"We couldn't find Ainsley, but we're here as Kayla's guests," Lu blurted out.

The woman looked at the three of them suspiciously.

"They're your guests, Kayla?" she asked.

Kayla nodded.

"All right, then," the secretary said, though she didn't seem happy about it. "That's one dollar each."

"Pay her," Lu said to Theo as she hurried Kayla into the gym.

Theo and the woman exchanged looks. Theo shrugged, and reached for his wallet.

The glowing, haunted orbs continued to swirl around the cavern. I caught brief glimpses of the faces in them. There were both men and women. All looked deadly serious.

"*Araba!*" Tomac shouted.

She had climbed up onto the altar and stood with her arms outstretched as if she wanted to hug those little, fiery witch-orbs. Whatever *Araba* meant, it was a signal. The floating lights gathered in the air above the altar, creating a circle over the witches' heads.

The chanting stopped. The witches looked up at the glowing circle with a mix of pride and awe as the witchy light bathed them in its evil warmth. The cavern had suddenly grown very quiet. All I could hear was the heavy breathing of the excited witches.

"It is time for our priestess to ascend," Tomac announced. She looked down at Ainsley and added, "This Samhain will forever be remembered as our new beginning, thanks to you. Now go."

The chanting kicked in again.

Ainsley stepped away from the altar, moving slowly as if in a fog, and walked straight for the tunnel that led to the school. She was headed for the dance!

With one last, desperate effort, I yanked on the rope that bound me to the pillar. The bottom of the column cracked. *Yes!* It was giving way! With two more violent tugs, I was able to pull the rope beneath the pillar. The force shifted the column ever so slightly, and dirt fell from the ceiling, where it was holding up the roof. Chunks of gravel rained down on me, and for a second I feared the whole ceiling would come crashing down. I covered my head, expecting the worst, but the beam held. Barely.

The witches had no idea what I was up to. They were all focused on Ainsley, who was halfway across the cavern on her way to the tunnel.

My wrists were still tied together, but I was free. I had to get out of there.

Ainsley seemed to know exactly what she was supposed to do. She continued to walk, trancelike, toward the archway and disappeared through the narrow opening.

Next stop . . . Fright Night.

The orbs bobbed in the air over Ainsley's head like supernatural escorts, lighting her way along the dark tunnel.

This was my chance. While all eyes were on her, I moved quickly in the other direction, toward the stairs that led up and out, into the clearing. I made sure to travel behind the row of wooden pillars in case any of the witches happened to look my way. The columns were spaced about five feet apart, plenty close enough for me to use them as shields. I made it to the stairs and climbed the steps two at a time, tripping and falling more than once on the uneven stone, but that didn't stop me. I made it out without being chased by any wolves or ravens or glowing orbs or witches.

What a nightmare.

When I popped up to the surface, the first thing I noticed was that night had fallen and the sky was alive with stars. Millions of stars. I don't remember ever seeing so many that clearly. Their light was so intensely bright that it lit up the forest like daytime. It may have been my imagination, but it felt as though the sky was charged with some kind of magical force.

Maybe because it was. And it was *bad* magic.

The second thing I noticed was that something felt off. I don't know why it took me more than a few seconds to figure out what it was because it was pretty obvious.

The ring of tall, dense brush that surrounded the coven's circle was gone. The pile of rocks that marked the entrance to the cavern was no longer hidden from the world. I couldn't help but think that was part of the program. The witches no longer needed their lair to be a secret, for once their plan was in motion, there would be no more hiding for them. They wanted everyone to know they existed. More witches would be coming, whether from other parts of the world or other dimensions and times. This was their meeting ground. It was cleared and ready.

The stage was set.

Unless we stopped Ainsley.

I took off running, through the woods, headed back for the school.

I sure hoped Lu and Theo had stopped the dance.

CHAPTER
15

*The Halloween dance had just begun and already
it was a crazy success.*

Unlike most school dance parties, where boys
and girls stood on opposite sides of the gym nervously waiting for someone to break the ice, the kids
of Coppell Middle School were ready for fun and
jumped right in. Perhaps their costumes gave them
self-confidence. Or it might have been because the
DJ knew his audience and kicked the dance off with
all the right music. Or maybe there was a mysterious, electric tension in the air that urged the kids to
let loose. Whatever the reason, Ainsley's dance was
already one they'd never forget.

And it was only getting started.

Theo and Lu moved through the crowded gym with Kayla right behind them. They scanned the crowd of costumed kids, searching for Ainsley.

"Everybody's got a mask on," Theo complained. "We'll never pick her out."

"This is bad," Lu said nervously. "We've got to clear this place."

She looked around frantically, then spotted something and charged through the crowd of dancers, headed for the far side of the gym.

Theo was about to follow when Kayla grabbed his arm and held him back. She looked at him imploringly, wanting to know what was going on.

"It's Ainsley," Theo said. "Everything that's happened, all the accidents. She caused them. But it wasn't her fault. She was being . . . manipulated."

Kayla's look of confusion only deepened.

"I know it's hard to understand, but she might try to do something bad tonight. A lot of kids could get hurt unless we stop her, so please, you have to leave right now."

Kayla shook her head adamantly. She wasn't budging.

Theo was stuck, and frustrated.

"Okay, then stay close to me."

He grabbed Kayla's hand and dragged her into the sea of dancers, trying to catch up with Lu.

Lu pushed her way through to the far side of the dance floor and broke out of the crowd. She looked around and quickly found what she wanted.

The fire alarm.

She steeled herself and went for it. The device was nothing more than a red switch on the wall with the word FIRE on it in bold white letters. Pulling the switch would break a small glass tube there to prevent the alarm from being triggered accidentally. Lu strode directly to the fire alarm, reached for the switch, curled her fingers around it, and held her breath as . . .

"Hello, Lu."

Lu spun around to face . . .

. . . Ainsley.

"What are you doing?" Ainsley asked sweetly, without a hint of tension or anger.

"Where's Marcus?" Lu asked, frantic.

Ainsley looked around as if searching for him.

"I don't know, he could be anywhere," Ainsley said. "Please don't touch that alarm."

"I know this isn't your fault," Lu said, breathless. "You can't help yourself. But I won't let you hurt anybody."

She spun back around and reached for the switch again.

She never touched it.

Her body suddenly went stiff, as if all of her muscles had seized at the same time. Her eyes went wide with surprise as she tried to open her mouth to speak, but no words came out. She had no control over her movements. Her body twisted around until her back hit the wall, next to the fire alarm.

Ainsley stood with one arm raised, her tensed fingers pointing at Lu, channeling the power of the coven. She had no expression. She didn't appear surprised or angry or sympathetic. It was as if Lu was nothing more than a minor problem to be dealt with.

"Sorry, Lu," Ainsley said casually, as if she wasn't sorry at all. "I can't let you do that. I have a responsibility."

Lu stood with her back against the wall, unable to move.

"But don't worry," Ainsley said brightly. "This won't take long."

She turned away from Lu to face the crowded gym. Slowly she raised her other arm, both palms facing up as if she were lifting a massive weight.

The gym lights flickered.

The orange Halloween lights strung across the ceiling blinked once, twice, then died.

The thumping dance music stopped abruptly.

A collective groan of annoyance went up from the kids.

The overhead lights flickered once more, then died, throwing the gym into near darkness.

There were gasps of confusion and a few surprised screams. Some kids laughed, but nervously. No doubt everyone was thinking the same thing:

Now what?

Seconds later, an emergency generator kicked in and restored power to the lights. A cheer went up, but it was only a tease. Within seconds the lights died again. But the gym didn't go dark. Filling the space was an eerie white glow that came from the light of countless stars, impossibly bright stars that looked down on the students through windows near the ceiling.

The kids stood still, nervous, not knowing what to do. It was a frozen moment between what was and what would be.

A faint rumbling filled the gym. It sounded like a distant fleet of monster trucks. The ominous sound quickly grew louder, making the windows rattle in their frames. Whatever was causing the noise was closing in. Fast.

The kids looked around with growing concern. They made eye contact with one another, but no one had any answers. They were all too stunned to move.

The rumbling sound transformed into movement. The gym floor began to vibrate. The vibration swiftly intensified into full-on shaking.

It was an earthquake.

That was enough to kick the kids into action. There was screaming as everyone ran for the exits. The dance had become a panicked mass of bodies desperate to escape.

Slam! Slam! Slam!

Every last exit door banged shut. When kids reached them and pushed on the bars, the doors didn't move.

They were trapped.

The shaking intensified. Some kids lost their balance and fell to the floor. Others continued to push against the doors, but it was futile. They were locked tight. Many kids ran for other exits only to find the same thing. Locked. It was the same with all of them. Nobody was getting out of that gym.

Crash! Crash!

The windows near the ceiling exploded, sending a shower of glass falling to the floor. The shards hit like hailstones, bouncing and scattering throughout the gym. Kids ran for cover, diving under tables or pressing themselves against the walls to avoid the deluge. They cried and screamed in fear and confusion, but there was no escape.

In the middle of it all was Ainsley.

As mayhem swirled around her, she walked serenely to the center of the gym. Her serene manner was in sharp contrast to the total chaos surrounding her. She was calm while everyone else was losing their minds.

Several kids spotted her.

They knew Ainsley.

Ainsley always had the answers.

They were drawn to her as if she were the savior who could lead them to safety.

As Ainsley stood at center court, the kids formed a wide circle around her not unlike the ring of brambles in the forest that circled the entrance to the coven's lair.

They were looking to her for help, unaware that she was the very cause of their terror.

Theo and Kayla ran to Lu, who stood with her back against the wall, frozen, staring straight ahead.

"What happened?" Theo yelled.

Lu couldn't answer.

Theo shook her shoulders.

Lu didn't respond. She was gone.

The responsibility of stopping Ainsley had fallen to Theo. He stole a quick glance at the mayhem in the gym, closed his eyes, then reached out and finished what Lu had started.

He pulled the fire alarm.

There was no sound. No alarm. No flashing lights. Theo could only hope that the alert had gone out and help would soon be on the way. But would it be too late?

"Stay with her," Theo ordered Kayla, and ran for Ainsley. He had to fight his way through the mass of kids surrounding her, pushing through them just as he had fought through the brambles that circled the witch's hollow, hoping to reach her before the disaster grew even worse.

Ainsley stood in the center of the circle of kids, turning slowly, making eye contact with those who stared back at her in wonder, hoping she would somehow stop the horror.

Theo broke through and into the circle.

"Ainsley!" he shouted. "Stop!"

The shaking stopped instantly. All was still. The gym grew deathly quiet.

Theo looked around with confusion as if he couldn't believe stopping Ainsley were as simple as that.

The kids could breathe again. There was a collective sigh of relief. They had dodged a bullet and the earthquake had passed without major damage. The only sounds were a few random whimpers and cries. The worst was over.

Until it wasn't.

Boom!

The wooden gym floor erupted. Ten feet from Ainsley, a massive, pointed rock drove up through the floor. Kids dove out of the way, pushing and shoving to get to safety.

Boom!

Another eruption exploded on the other side of the gym as a mass of solid, sharp Massachusetts granite thrust up toward the ceiling. The sound of violently splintering wood drowned out the screams of the terrified kids.

The earthquake had come back with a vengeance. It tore the basketball court floor apart right under the feet of hundreds of victims ... the sacrificial lambs of the Black Moon Circle. They were seconds away from plunging into the chaos below.

Ainsley was the only person not panicking. While the others scrambled futilely to find safety, she stood calmly at center court with her arms raised, channeling the power of the coven to rile the destructive forces of nature.

"Ainsley, stop it!" Theo shouted, and started toward her.

Ainsley casually flicked a finger his way. Instantly, the gym floor in Theo's path splintered and broke apart to reveal a deep chasm.

Theo put on the brakes, but his leather-soled shoes skidded on the slick court. He tried to resist, but his momentum was too strong. He was headed straight for the rift and about to become the first casualty.

"Gotcha!"

Theo was tackled hard and knocked back from the abyss, hitting the floor with a bone-jarring thud. He looked up at the guy who had saved him.

"We're not going down that easy," his savior said.

Marcus O'Mara had arrived at the dance.

———————

CHAPTER
16

I sprinted away from the hollow and back through the woods, headed for the school, with only the light from the freakish stars to guide me. I kept working at the rope around my wrists, which wasn't easy while running, but I finally got the knots untied. The whole time I kept looking around for fear a tree might reach down and grab me or vines would snake out and wrap themselves around my ankles. None of that happened. Either the witches didn't know I was gone, or they didn't care because I was already too late.

I blasted out of the forest and sprinted for the gym, following the thumping bass sound. I rounded the building and was nearly there when I saw the lights flicker inside. Then the music died. I knew it couldn't be a coincidence. Ainsley was there and doing the coven's dirty work.

A few kids in zombie costumes came running out, looking as though they wanted to be anywhere else but there. Fright Night. Yeah, exactly.

"What's going on?" I called to some kid wearing a Superman costume.

"I don't know," he called back in a shaky voice. "The place is falling apart."

So much for Superman saving the day.

As I ran for the gym, I saw Nate sitting on his three-wheeled ATV near the entrance. It didn't look as though he had even tried to go into the dance. Lucky for him.

"What the heck?" I asked.

"I don't know," he said in a panicked voice that was two octaves above normal. "It sounds like the whole place is coming down. I swear I had nothing to do with it."

Another giant FRIGHT NIGHT banner hung over the doors. Whoever put that up had no idea how true those words were going to be.

I looked to Nate, and to his ATV. An idea was forming. A desperate idea, but still an idea.

"Don't go anywhere, all right?" I called to him as I continued toward the gym.

"Why?" he asked. "So the cops can blame this on me?"

"No. So you can help end this, and maybe prove you're innocent."

Nate had no comeback and I didn't wait for him to think of one. I sprinted into the building, through the lobby, and straight into the gym. The second my feet hit the wooden floor I felt it rumbling like an earthquake. Nothing like that was going on outside. Whatever was happening, it was focused on the gym.

I stood frozen a few feet inside the entrance, when all the doors suddenly slammed shut. Instinctively, I spun back to try and reopen them, but they were locked tight. If I had gotten there only a few seconds later, I would have been trapped outside. Now I was trapped inside. I wasn't so sure which was worse. A few seconds later, the windows near the ceiling exploded, sending thousands of tiny bits of glass crashing to the floor.

Being in the gym was worse.

I didn't know which way to turn or what to do. That's when the shaking stopped. No sooner did I think the worst was over than the gym floor exploded in several places, giving way to sharp rock spires that drove up from below.

The coven's plan was coming clear. They were going to wipe out every last kid in that gym. That was the sacrifice. Their presence would be announced to the world by a horrifying act that would prove their ability to control nature and dominate the human race.

And they were doing it all through Ainsley.

Ainsley.

She stood at center court in a circle of kids, calmly holding her arms out as she channeled the evil power of the coven to make the ground come alive.

I saw Theo break from the crowd on the opposite side of the gym and run for her.

"Ainsley, stop it!" he shouted.

That couldn't be good. If she had the power to tear the gym apart, who knows what she'd do to Theo if he interfered. Without a second thought, I ran for him, hoping to stop him before Ainsley turned her destructive power on him. I was halfway across the empty stretch of gym when the floor broke apart and opened up in front of Theo. Ainsley wasn't going to let him get close to her. If I had more than half a second to think about it, I probably wouldn't have done what I did. But all I saw was my friend headed toward his doom. I sprinted forward and dove across the chasm, locked in on Theo.

"Gotcha!" I shouted.

I tackled him, hard, and the two of us tumbled to the floor. Safe. For a second, anyway.

"We're not going down that easy," I said.

Theo's eyes were wide and wild. He knew how close he'd come to falling into the abyss.

"It's about t-t-time you got here," he stammered.

I scrambled to my feet, helped Theo up, and backed away from the chasm.

Ainsley stood, her arms outstretched, a serene look on her face as she gazed skyward. The gym was about to come crashing down on all of us, including her, and she couldn't have cared less. The reign of the high priestess would be a short one. She was just another sacrifice. Her death would no doubt release the magic she'd been incubating so it could return to the original owners . . . a hundred times more powerful.

All around us, kids cowered in fear as the floor jumped and the walls cracked. Soon the heavy steel girders that held up the ceiling would buckle and fall. Nowhere was safe.

I looked up to see several of the glowing spirit-orbs floating in through the broken windows to hover near the ceiling and observe their high priestess from above. They were there to witness the revenge of their coven, and the sacrifice that would bring about its rebirth.

I didn't know what to do.

But somebody did.

"Ainsley, stop it right now!"

The bold voice cut through the rumbling and cracking.

It wasn't me. Or Theo. Or any of the kids who were whimpering and hugging one another.

It was Kayla.

She was on Ainsley's side of the chasm, walking slowly toward her. It was a surreal sight to see this shy girl dressed as a princess walking straight and tall, showing no fear, while everyone else cowered.

Oh yeah, and she was talking.

"Please don't do this," she called out in a calm, sweet voice that none of the kids had ever heard before.

It got Ainsley's attention.

Her face had been lifted toward the ceiling, but when she heard Kayla's voice, she dropped her chin, and her eyes snapped open in surprise, as if hearing Kayla's voice was an outrageously impossible event. Because it was.

"You always tried to protect me," Kayla said. "Now I want to protect you. Stop this before someone gets hurt."

Ainsley stared at Kayla with a look of total confusion. I couldn't tell if she understood what Kayla was saying, or if she was stunned because Kayla was saying anything at all.

Above us, the glowing orbs grew brighter. I don't

think anybody else in the gym noticed, or cared. They were too busy being terrified out of their minds.

But I saw it.

The witches weren't happy.

Ainsley dropped her arms. Her entire body relaxed, as though she had been released from the powerful hold of the coven.

"Kayla?" she said. "You have such a sweet voice."

Kayla smiled and shrugged.

The shaking slowly weakened. The floor felt solid again. The screeching, tearing sounds of the gym being ripped apart echoed into silence. None of the hundreds of kids who were scattered everywhere dared move.

Kayla approached Ainsley, slowly but confidently.

Ainsley shot quick, confused glances around the gym as if she was seeing it all for the first time.

"What's going on?" she asked, her voice shaking with fear. "How did I get here?"

Kayla stepped up and took her hands.

"I don't know," Kayla said soothingly. "Keep looking at me. Listen to my voice. Whatever was happening here, we can't let it start again."

Tears grew in Ainsley's eyes as she nodded in agreement.

The room suddenly grew bright as the overhead lights came back on with full power. The orange

Halloween lights glowed once again and the DJ's dance music boomed to life. The upbeat party music was an odd soundtrack to the scene of terror and destruction.

The exit doors flew open on their own, prompting a stampede of kids desperate to escape.

"What the heck?" Lu said as she ran up to us.

"You're okay?" Theo asked.

"I think. I've never been paralyzed before. I don't want it to happen again."

The overhead lights grew bright. Brighter than normal. The huge room was lit up like it was daytime. I looked up to see the brilliant glow wasn't coming just from the gym lighting. The multiple spirit-lights looked burning hot, as if enraged by Ainsley's failure. They darted around like a swarm of angry bees, then suddenly swooped down as one and flew onto the stage and past the DJ, who dove out of the way. As the DJ hit the ground, the orbs kept moving and disappeared backstage.

"Uh . . . what was that?" Lu asked.

"That was bad news," I said. "The spell over Ainsley might be broken, but the coven is still in business."

I grabbed Theo by the shoulders and said, "Stay with Ainsley and Kayla. Don't let Ainsley leave. Sit on her if you have to. Just keep her here."

I pointed to Lu and said, "Come with me."

"Where are we going?"

"On a witch hunt," I said, and sprinted for the exit with Lu right behind me.

We fought our way out of there along with the hundreds of other kids.

"Witch hunt?" Lu called to me over the din of the multitude of people we were swimming along with.

"The coven's been building up to this for years," I said. "No way the witches are done. I think they'll come after Ainsley again."

"So how can we stop it?" she asked.

"We do what the books said and crush the core of their power."

"Uh, you know how to do that?" Lu asked suspiciously.

"I have a pretty good idea," I said.

We finally made it outside to see a bunch of fire trucks screaming up. There wasn't any fire, but the gym was a wreck. No way it was safe. The fire department would make sure everybody got out and then seal it off.

We heard people shouting to the firefighters that the school had been hit by an intense earthquake. Nobody thought there was anything mystical going on or that Ainsley had anything to do with it. Just as well. It was way easier for people to believe a natural disaster like an earthquake had struck rather than that they had been targeted by a centuries-old supernatural force.

We jumped out of the flow of fleeing kids and I scanned the parking lot.

"What are you looking for?" Lu asked.

"Our last best hope."

I spotted him sitting on his bike, watching the chaos with wide eyes.

"Nate Christmas?" Lu asked, incredulous. "The delinquent is our last best hope?"

"Hey, some of my best friends are delinquents."

"Yeah, mine too," she said, staring right at me.

We ran for him.

"What the hell?" Nate asked, totally amped up.

"Earthquake," I said. "It's over."

"It's a mess," he said. "I know I'm going to get blamed for this."

"You want me to bail you out?" I said. "If you help us I'll make sure everybody knows you had nothing to do with this or any of the other disasters at school. I can even make you a hero."

"Yeah?" he said skeptically. "What do I have to do?"

"Just cause a little mayhem," I replied.

Nate looked me square in the eyes as if trying to decide whether he believed me.

"You know, I don't really care what people think about me," he said, then smiled slyly. "But I like mayhem."

We were in business.

CHAPTER
17

"Look out below!" Nate called.

He had climbed up onto the balcony over the front entrance of the school to cut down the FRIGHT NIGHT banner. The huge vinyl sign hit the ground and I quickly grabbed it, separating it from the strong climbing ropes that had been used to tie it up.

"Coil the other rope," I called to Lu.

She swept up the second rope and began to coil it.

"What's the point?" she asked.

"It's all about the altar," I said. "It's the center of the coven's power. That's what Everett read in all the other books. If we destroy it, it'll end their powers."

"We can do that with rope?" Lu asked, incredulous.

"I sure hope so."

I took the coiled rope from Lu and lashed it together with the other coil to create one superlong length of rope.

"Now what?" Nate asked as he rejoined us.

"We go to the woods," I said. "Back to where you were lighting off M-80s."

Nate's eyes grew wide. "How'd you know about that?"

"I was there. You saved my butt. Now you're going to do the same for the rest of humanity."

Nate scowled. "You are one very strange dude."

"You have no idea."

Nate jumped onto the ATV.

"Sweet ride," Lu said, admiring the three-wheeled bike. "You a rich kid?"

"Nah, I'm a kid with parents who feel guilty about never being around. So they buy me stuff."

Once again I felt bad for Nate Christmas. The guy had issues. But it wasn't the time for anybody to bare their soul. Besides, at that moment I was kind of happy his parents had gotten him an ATV, whatever the reason.

Lu sat on the seat behind Nate, and I squeezed on behind her. It was a tight fit, but we had to make it work. It was especially tricky because I had a heavy coil of climbing rope around my shoulder.

"Don't take your time," I said.

"Don't worry," Nate replied, and hit the throttle.

If I hadn't grabbed on to Lu I would have been thrown off the back. She had Nate in a bear hug and I had my arms wrapped around both of them. We sped around the corner of the gym, shot across the back parking lot, and bounced over the curb onto the grass, heading for the woods.

Again.

I kept looking down at the grass, fearing it would magically grow tall and try to tangle us up, but we blasted across with no problem. Once we got into the woods, Nate had to make a couple of sharp turns to avoid the trees that had fallen when the witches tried to take me out.

"What the hell happened here?" Nate called over the whine of the engine.

"Another earthquake!" I shouted back. I didn't think it would be smart to answer "witchcraft"; he might have turned the bike around and killed my plan.

The fallen trees were proof that what had happened wasn't a dream or a Boggin-like illusion, but they gave me serious doubts about what we were headed toward. The witches weren't kidding around. I could be leading us straight into disaster. But I didn't know what else to do.

After a breakneck ride through the woods, aided by

light from the skyful of brilliant stars, we arrived at the clearing. Nate rolled to a stop several yards from the pile of boulders that marked the entrance to the underground cavern.

"I don't get it," he said. "There was a big wall of bushes here. We must be in the wrong spot."

"It's the right spot," I said as I got off the bike. "The bushes are gone."

"How can they just be gone?" Nate asked, sounding a little shaken.

"Let it go," I replied. "It's the *least* impossible thing you're going to see. You sure you're up for this?"

"Yeah, yeah, sure," he said defensively. "But—"

"Kill the engine," I commanded.

Nate turned off the ATV's engine and the forest became deathly silent.

"Now what?" Lu asked. She sounded even more nervous than Nate.

"Let's push the bike close to those rocks," I said.

Nate put the vehicle into neutral, and the three of us pushed it into the clearing.

"I don't know who you are or what we're doing here," Nate whispered, "but I like it."

I put my finger to my lips to tell him to keep quiet.

We pushed the bike up to the rocks so that its back end was close to the first giant boulder. Without a word,

I pulled the coiled rope off my shoulder and tied one end around the bike frame toward the rear.

"There's a cavern down below," I whispered. "The ceiling is held up by rotten wooden pillars. I'm going to go down there and tie the other end of the rope to the columns. Lu, you stay by the opening and make sure the rope doesn't get caught on anything. Nate, you stay with the bike. Lu, when the rope is set, I'll signal you to signal Nate. Nate, you fire up the engine and gun it out of here."

"So we yank out the pillars?" Nate asked with a devilish gleam in his eyes.

"Exactly. I'm thinking the whole cavern will collapse."

"And destroy the altar," Lu whispered with a sly smile. "Awesome."

"Let's hope it works," I said. "Because if it doesn't . . ."

I didn't finish the sentence.

"This better not wreck my bike," Nate said.

"Your bike'll be fine. The wood is so rotten it would fall down if you sneezed on it."

"This is what's gonna make me a hero?" Nate asked.

"Absolutely," I answered with confidence. "They'll probably erect a statue of you."

Nate beamed. "I'd be good with that."

I quickly moved toward the rock pile, paying out the rope. Lu stayed right with me.

"A statue?" she asked quietly.

"It's all I could think of."

We climbed up onto the massive, moss-covered boulders, making sure the rope didn't get caught on anything. Then we slipped down the other side, where we stood near the opening at the top of the rock stairs.

"Stay right here," I whispered.

"I want to come."

"No, you've got to be out here to make sure the rope doesn't catch on anything once it goes taut."

Truth was, as much as I wanted Lu with me in case something went wrong, I also didn't want her going down into the witches' hollow. There was no sense in both of us risking our necks.

"Are you sure?" she asked.

"Yes. Be ready in case I call for you to get Nate moving."

"With you still down there?"

"I'll be out a few seconds later, don't worry. But every second may count."

"Okay," she said, though I knew she'd rather be going down with me. "Be careful."

I cautiously made my way down the stairs, letting out the rope as I went. I descended through pitch darkness for a few seconds, moving from starlight above to candlelight below. I had no idea what to expect. My hope was that the witches were still caught up in their trance and wouldn't notice me creeping around.

On the other hand, my fear was that they were standing around, pissed off, knowing their plan had failed and looking for somebody to take their anger out on.

I reached the bottom and cautiously poked my head around the corner to see . . . nothing. The cavern was empty. The candles on the altar were still lit, but there wasn't a witch in sight. My hopes skyrocketed. The coven had lost. They thought they had total control of Ainsley, but they didn't count on her conscience being stronger than their magic.

All it took was for Kayla to speak.

Ainsley would never be their high priestess or their sacrifice.

But it still wasn't over. The witches were patient. They had been trying to get their revenge for more than a couple hundred years. I had no doubt that they would set their sights on another Ainsley in the future and once again try to rain terror down on the people of Coppell.

But that wouldn't happen if I destroyed the altar for good.

I still had several yards of rope left and went to work quickly. I wound the rope once around the nearest pillar, then moved to the next one. By the time I ran out of rope, I had looped it around six of the columns. Most important, the last one was next to the altar. If this worked and the cavern caved in, the altar would be buried under tons of rock.

That was a big if. I had to hope that the wooden pillars were as rotten as the one I had sawn through.

I was ready to get the heck out of there, when I realized I was standing right next to the altar. I couldn't help but stare at the ancient artifacts on it. The candles and plates and brass holders were hundreds of years old. And they were magic. I'd seen it. I believed. It was incredible to think that the witches could use chants and incantations to control nature. And people. They really were some kind of higher beings. But their power was corrupt. They used it to manipulate and destroy. They may have been able to control the natural world, but there was nothing natural about what they were doing. It was evil. There was no other word for it. They were evil and had to be stopped.

I walked up to the altar, feeling the warmth on my face that came from the multitude of candles. It was sort of hypnotic. I gazed at the flames, looking over the extensive array, and saw something that made me gasp with surprise. I had to blink to make sure I wasn't seeing things as I leaned in close to get a better look.

There was no mistake. Small faces were gazing back at me from inside each of the individual flames. I guess

I should have been scared, but after all I'd seen, nothing freaked me out anymore. But it sure as heck was eerie. I could make out enough detail in each face to see that there were men and women of all ages. Some men had beards; some wore glasses. My eye caught movement in one of the shiny brass plates. I focused on it and saw a woman's face looking back at me as if her image was being reflected in the metal surface. I whipped around, expecting to see somebody behind me, but nobody was there. The witch wasn't in the cavern—she was in the plate.

I saw more faces in the other brass plates, just like with the flames. Every shiny surface held a spirit. Or witch. It was like the items were charged with the magic of witchcraft.

The long silver dagger that Tomac had used to cut Ainsley rested in the center of the altar. I looked into its shiny surface but didn't see a face. What was different about this one thing? It was the one unique item on the table. Tomac had used it in the witches' horrible ceremony. Why wasn't there a face in it?

"Did you really think this was over?" came an all-too-familiar voice.

I spun toward the tunnel that led back to the school to see Tomac standing there.

She wasn't alone.

Ainsley was with her.

"WHAT'S TAKING HIM?" NATE called to Lu.

Lu didn't answer. She was too busy staring down into the dark cave and wondering the exact same thing.

Nate was getting antsy.

"This is starting to feel stupid," he said. "I can't believe I went along with you idiots."

He got off his bike and walked to the rear.

"I'm done," he said, and knelt down to untie the rope. "Tell O'Mara I don't care if he helps me out or—"

He was cut off by the sound of a howling wolf.

Lu stood up straight. "Uh-oh," she whispered.

Another howl joined the first, followed by another, and another.

Lu jumped up onto a boulder where she could see into the woods.

"No way," Nate said nervously. "There aren't any wolves around here. Are there?"

"Uh," Lu stammered, "n-n-no. I don't know. Maybe."

"Forget this," Nate said, and started to release the rope.

Lu saw what he was doing and bounded down off the rocks. "Don't! This is our only hope of stopping—"

"Christmas!" bellowed a man's voice.

Lu and Nate froze. Busted. But by who?

They both slowly looked to where the wall of bushes used to be to see . . .

"Mr. Martin?" Nate called out, confused.

The teacher slowly stalked toward them.

"And the new girl," Martin added with disdain. "I thought I took care of you."

"I am in such trouble," Nate said.

"You have no idea," Lu replied.

"Look, Martin, uh, Mr. Martin," Nate said. "I don't know anything about what's going on here. I just followed these clowns because they said we were going to have some fun. None of this was my idea."

"Clowns?" Martin said as he drew closer. "Who else is here?"

"Shut up, Nate," Lu said under her breath.

"I don't want any trouble," Nate said as he edged toward the seat of his bike. "I'm gonna take off before something bad happens."

Martin chuckled. "I'm afraid it's too late for that."

There was movement in the deep moon shadows beneath the trees.

"What . . . the hell . . . is that?" Nate whined.

"I think that's the trouble he was talking about," Lu replied.

Appearing from out of the shadows was a line of wolves. Their fur glowed in the moonlight, along with their eyes ... eyes that were focused on Lu and Nate. Dozens appeared from every direction. The animals formed a circle that slowly tightened as they stalked closer.

"This isn't happening," Nate said with growing panic.

"The ascension didn't go as planned," Martin said calmly. "But it doesn't matter. The coven will not be denied. There are hundreds of confused children in the parking lot. One way or another, there will be a sacrifice tonight ... beginning right here."

Tomac pulled Ainsley closer to the altar.

"Ainsley, are you okay?" I called out.

"What is going on, Marcus?" she cried. "Ms. Tomac said she was taking me somewhere safe."

Ainsley wasn't under the witch's spell. There was still hope.

"Don't listen to her," I said. "She's not who you think she is."

"And who am I, Marcus?" Tomac said. "Explain it to her."

"She's a witch," I said. "There's no other way to say it. She got in your head. None of what happened is your fault. It's all her and her coven."

"I—I don't understand," Ainsley stammered.

"Nothing has changed," Tomac said to me while keeping a firm grip on Ainsley's arm. "The ascension will continue."

"What is she talking about?" Ainsley begged.

"She wants revenge," I said. "For something that happened hundreds of years ago. She thinks her coven is all-powerful but it isn't."

"Keep telling yourself that," Tomac scoffed.

"It's true," I said. "You were stopped. Not by magic or supernatural power. You were beaten by a couple of girls who cared about each other. Simple as that. No matter what happens tonight, you're always going to be fighting human nature. That's a fight you'll never win."

Tomac stiffened as if I'd hit a nerve. Ainsley struggled to get away, but Tomac held her tight.

"You believe we've been stopped?" she said icily. "Even as we stand here, the coven is exacting its revenge. Human nature is no match for the centuries we've spent learning to manipulate true nature."

Her words stunned me. What was going on out there? Is that why the coven wasn't in the cavern? Were they going after the kids who had escaped from the gym?

THE CIRCLE OF WOLVES grew tighter around Lu and Nate. The animals' low growls joined to create the sound of an infernal engine that was slowly powering up.

"Have to admit," Martin said, "I'm thrilled you're going to be the first victim, Christmas. I really don't like you."

"What did you get me into?" Nate whined to Lu.

Lu took a defiant step closer to Martin.

"What about your high priestess?" she said boldly. "She didn't go through with the plan."

Martin shrugged. "She'll still serve her purpose. Our powers grew within her for years and we'll get them back a hundred times more potent ... at the moment of her sacrifice."

Lu looked shaken. She took a step back toward Nate and whispered, "Start the motor."

Nate was too frightened to move.

"Do it," Lu seethed under her breath.

Nate snapped back into the moment. He jumped onto his ATV and fired up the engine.

Martin laughed. "Really? How far do you think you'll get?"

Lu glanced back at the pile of rocks that concealed the entrance to the cavern. Marcus was still down there. No signal had been given. If she and Nate took off, Marcus would be crushed beneath a ton of rocks. But if they didn't at least try to escape there would be no hope of destroying the altar. The coven would be more powerful than ever, and there was no telling how many kids at the school would be hunted down and attacked by the pack of angry wolves.

"What do I do?" Nate whined.

I looked to the altar and saw dozens of tiny spirit faces staring back at me from the flames. They were in total command. The coven was about to get its revenge and all I could do was stand there . . .

. . . with a rope attached to the rotten pillars that could bring the whole thing down. Only trouble was, it would all come down on Ainsley and me.

I grabbed the silver dagger off the altar and held it out toward Tomac threateningly. It was a totally desperate move. I had no idea what to do with it.

"Let her go" were the only lame words I could come up with.

Tomac's reaction surprised me. She looked shaken. Seriously shaken. Huh? No way she believed I could do any real damage with that knife.

"Put that down," she commanded in a shaky voice.

She was truly rattled. Which made me think there might be a lot more to this knife than I thought. It was the key tool she had used during their ceremony. It was the only magical item on the table that didn't hold a witch's spirit. Did this thing have power of its own? I didn't put it down. Instead, I held the dagger up higher.

"I said, let her go." I spoke with more authority this time.

"And I said put it down," Tomac commanded, though her voice was quivering.

Up until that moment, Tomac had shown nothing but confidence. Now she was nervous as all heck. It had to be the dagger, because she sure wasn't afraid of me.

"Let Ainsley go," I said, trying to sound more confident than I felt.

"She stays," Tomac replied. "But you can save yourself. Put that down and I'll allow you to return to your little library."

I looked at my own reflection in the dagger's silver blade. I definitely had some control. No way I was giving it up.

"Maybe I should take this with me," I taunted her.

"No!" Tomac screamed. "You will suffer for desecrating the totem!"

Totem? Interesting.

"This thing means a lot to you, huh?" I asked.

Tomac didn't reply, but her eyes said it all.

"If I'm in trouble for messing with it, I might as well make this worthwhile."

I gingerly grasped the tip of the blade in one hand while firmly holding the handle with the other.

"Stop," Tomac hissed through clenched teeth.

I raised the dagger over my head.

"You will not!" Tomac screamed.

"Yeah I will," I replied.

She let go of Ainsley and lunged at me.

I brought the dagger down hard on the edge of the altar. The moment the blade hit the stone, it snapped in two . . .

. . . and the world went insane.

Tomac let out a guttural cry as if I'd broken the knife on her head. She fell to her knees in anguish.

Ainsley ran to me, grabbed my arm, and held tight. We backed away from the altar as the candle flames glowed brighter. Each individual flame lifted up off its wick and floated toward the ceiling. The faces of the witches within them were contorted with expressions of agony, the same as Tomac's.

Whatever this knife was, whatever dark magic it held, it connected the entire coven.

Until I broke it.

THE WOLVES STOPPED MOVING.

Martin froze, as if he had been hit by a shot of electricity. He stood still for a moment, then dropped to the ground, writhing in torment.

"What the—?" Nate mumbled.

The wolves backed off and they too fell to the ground, pawing at their ears as if listening to a shrill, painful dog whistle. They all wailed out a chilling sound that was somewhere between a howl and a human cry of agony.

Martin continued writhing in the dirt. His body twisted and cracked until it had transformed into a white wolf.

"Oh, that's not right!" Nate cried in shock.

Lu scrambled back up onto the rock pile.

"Marcus!" she screamed. "Get out of there!"

Ainsley and I stood mesmerized by the sight of the glowing, pained faces that rose toward the cavern's ceiling.

"Look!" Ainsley said, pulling my arm and gesturing at Tomac.

The witch was transforming. Her body first turned to shadow, then changed shape, and began to glow. Within seconds she had turned into a floating orb of light like all the others. As it rose toward the ceiling, I could see Tomac's face within the light, staring down at me in anguish and anger.

"Marcus! Get out of there!" came a voice from nowhere.

"Who is that?" Ainsley asked.

"Lu!" I exclaimed. Her voice brought me back into the moment. "We gotta go."

I pulled Ainsley toward the stairs.

THE WOLVES CONTINUED TO writhe in pain but fell silent as their twisted bodies turned to shadow and lifted off the ground, only to transform again. Light sprang from the center of each shadow, enveloping it and turning it into a floating flame. Within the flames, the witches' faces could be seen, contorted in misery.

I ran across the cavern, pulling Ainsley along, desperate to get out of there.

"Do it, Lu!" I screamed. "Go, go, go!"

THAT WAS THE SIGNAL.

Lu bounded down off the rocks, headed for the ATV.

"Go!" she screamed at Nate. "Now!"

Nate didn't have to be told twice. The moment Lu landed on the back of the ATV, he hit the throttle and the bike launched forward. The rope went taut, and held the bike back.

"Not enough power!" Nate called over the engine's whine.

The two rear wheels spun in the dirt as the front wheel lifted off the ground. The bike strained against the rope but didn't move.

"Oh my God, look!" Lu screamed.

The floating lights transformed once again. Each glowing flame was snuffed out as the witches took on a new form.

"White ravens," Lu gasped.

Every last flame turned into a huge white bird. The flock drew together, flew high above the clearing, then, as if choreographed, swooped down as one, headed toward Lu and Nate. The two ducked as the flock swept over their heads and continued toward the rock pile.

The witches had regained control.

"They're going for the hollow!" Lu exclaimed.

The flock flew tightly together, like a white-feathered missile. They rose above the boulders, then dove again and disappeared into the cave.

At that exact moment, the tires of the ATV finally

caught. The front wheel hit the ground and the bike shot forward.

"Yeah!" Nate shouted.

As Ainsley and I ran across the cavern, I saw the rope go taut. Yes! But the pillars held. The bike wasn't powerful enough to break the first one. The way I had looped them together, if the first one didn't break, the others wouldn't even get the chance.

"Keep going, get out of here!" I shouted to Ainsley. I pushed her toward the stairs, and then rushed to the first column.

The rope was as tight as a guitar string. Nate must have been gunning the engine, but it still wasn't enough. I kicked at the pillar with my heel. The wood was soft, but it wasn't giving up. Not without a fight. I gave it a few more kicks and heard a crack. It was going to go.

"Marcus, c'mon!" Ainsley wailed.

She hadn't left.

I continued kicking at the pillar.

"Just . . . one . . . more—"

Bang!

The column cracked at its base and was yanked away. Once it was loose, the energy of the rope was transferred to the next in line. It wasn't as strong, and it pulled away instantly. The dominoes were falling.

269

Dirt and gravel rained down. The ceiling was about to collapse.

I ran back to Ainsley.

"We're outta here!" I screamed, and pushed her toward the stairs.

We didn't get far.

Before we made it through the archway, a flock of screeching white ravens came flying down from above.

Ainsley screamed and pushed me back into the cavern.

The angry birds filled the hollow, screeching and wailing while diving at us.

The flames that had been hovering over the unholy site winked out as each of the floating witches turned into a raven. Whatever magic was broken with the dagger, the witches had found a way to fight past it by transforming into the hideous birds. The cavern was filled with a blur of white chaos . . .

. . . while, one after another, the wooden pillars were torn from their bases. They slammed into one another like bowling pins as the rope yanked them across the dirt floor. Ainsley and I had to dive out of the way or we would have been cut down by the careening lengths of wood and the rope that was pulling them along.

It was exactly what I had hoped for.

The ceiling collapsed.

Dirt and rocks fell all around us.

The flock of white ravens flew up in a desperate attempt to hold back the avalanche. They squawked and screamed and tried to join together, but all they managed to do was get hit by tumbling rocks. It was useless. The seat of the coven's power, its altar, was about to be buried.

And we were going to be buried along with it. I grabbed Ainsley's hand and started back for the stairs but stopped when I saw a frightening sight, something I hadn't counted on. The beams that had been dragged across the ground were jammed up in the archway, blocking the way out. The exit was sealed.

We were trapped.

I went into brain lock. There was nowhere to hide from the falling debris. In seconds we'd be buried, along with the coven of the Black Moon Circle.

"Come on!" Ainsley screamed.

She pulled me in the opposite direction from the blocked stairs, deeper into the cavern.

"No! What are you doing?" I yelled, near panic.

"The tunnel to the school!" she yelled back.

It was the first clear thought she'd had that entire day, and it couldn't have come at a better time.

We dodged through the mayhem as rocks and timber crashed down around us and the white ravens squawked overhead. As we passed the altar, a massive boulder fell from above and landed squarely on top of it. The stone legs blew out; the altar cracked in two and crumbled under a deluge of dirt and rocks, along with every last enchanted item the witches used to cast their spells and spread their evil.

I was hit on the shoulder by a falling stone, which brought me right back into the moment, and the danger we were still in.

"Keep moving!" Ainsley commanded.

We each held up one arm to protect our heads while holding hands to stay together. We made it to the tunnel and ducked through the archway but didn't stop there. There was no way to know if the destruction would continue and collapse the ancient passage between the hollow and the school. So we kept running. It was pitch dark, but better to fly blind than to be caught in the maelstrom. The farther we got, the fainter the sound of the collapsing cavern became. But we kept moving until the moment when we heard an earth-shattering crash that signaled the final implosion of the coven's hollow. The force of the crash was so violent that the ground shook. We stopped, held on to the wall to get our balance, and waited.

The sound of falling rocks ended. Nothing was

coming down on our heads. We were in total darkness surrounded by eerie silence.

"Are you okay?" I finally asked, gulping air.

"Marcus?" Ainsley said, just as winded.

"Yeah?"

"Good. I thought that was you."

"Uhhh . . . who else would it be?"

"I don't know," she said. "Where are we?"

"In the tunnel between the cavern and the school."

"The what?" she asked, sounding totally surprised.

"The tunnel," I replied. "You know. The same tunnel Tomac brought you through."

"Ms. Tomac?" Ainsley asked. "The librarian?"

"Yes! Don't you remember?"

There was a long moment of dark silence until Ainsley said, "No. I don't. I don't have any idea how I got here."

And with that, Ainsley's connection to the Black Moon Circle—and any memory of it—was gone.

Forever.

CHAPTER
18

Ainsley and I made our way back through the dark tunnel to the basement of the school.

It was slow going because we had to feel our way along in the dark. She didn't say a word or ask about anything that had happened. I think she was stunned into silence. Just as well. I didn't know what to say to her anyway.

I couldn't imagine what we would find back at the school. There was no way to know how far the Black Moon Circle had gotten with its evil plan before we destroyed the altar. Part of me didn't want to know. I was afraid that things might be pretty ugly.

After what seemed like hours, we finally saw light ahead of us. We had passed through the archway from the ancient tunnel and into the old foundation of the school, where a couple of overhead lightbulbs were burning.

"I'm really scared, Marcus," Ainsley finally said.

"Don't be," I said reassuringly. "Everything's going to be okay."

I'm not sure if I was trying to convince her or myself.

We climbed up out of the basement and headed straight for the gym. The lights were on, but they were dim. The school must have been using an emergency generator. It made the already spooky, ancient corridors even creepier. My heart started pounding hard as we drew closer to the gym, because I truly feared the worst.

Ainsley stuck to me like a magnet. She gripped my arm with both hands and peered over my shoulder as if I could offer some sort of protection.

When we entered the gym, we were faced with a scene of total destruction. The glass in all the windows near the ceiling had blown out. The gym floor looked more like a battlefield than a basketball court. Huge chunks of granite, pushed up from below, reached nearly all the way to the ceiling. Several chasms dropped down to who knows how deep. Most of the wooden floor was nothing more than a jumble of splinters. The impossible scene was made all the more so because of the eerie silence.

What we didn't see were people. It gave me hope that everyone had gotten out safely.

"Dude!" came a shaky voice.

We spun toward the stage, where the sound equipment was set up. From behind a large speaker, the DJ peered at us with wide, frightened eyes.

"Gotta hand it to you," he said, his voice shaking. "You guys really know how to throw a Halloween party."

I might think back and laugh at that someday. But probably not.

Ainsley surveyed the carnage, totally bewildered, and asked the obvious question: "What happened?"

How was I supposed to answer that? If she truly had no memory of the witches, it wasn't something I could sum up in one quick and neat answer.

"I'm not sure," I answered noncommittally. "Let's get outside."

We carefully picked our way across the destroyed gym to the main exit. As we got closer to the doors, we heard noises. There was life outside. We heard people talking, car doors slamming, distant sirens, and the squawk of walkie-talkies. We made it to the exit and looked out onto the parking lot, which was a scene of organized chaos. Emergency vehicles were everywhere. Fire engines, ambulances, and police cars filled the lot, their blue and red lights flashing.

Kids in costume were scattered about. Some were huddled together and crying while just as many wandered around aimlessly, as if in shock. Others were gathered in groups, recounting their experiences with adrenaline-fueled enthusiasm. Many kids were being treated by emergency medical people. There were a lot of bandages and temporary splints, but I didn't see any truly horrible injuries . . . or covered bodies on stretchers. My hopes rose that nobody had been seriously hurt or killed.

In other words, there had been no sacrifices.

"Marcus!"

Theo ran up to us along with Kayla, who was still wearing her princess costume. The two were holding hands.

"Oh man, thank God you're okay," Theo said.

"What happened, Theo?" I asked.

He knew exactly what I was going for.

"I know, I know," he answered quickly. "It was chaos, Marcus. Kids were running around and fire engines were screaming up and, oh yeah, the gym was falling apart. I looked away for five seconds, that's all. And Ainsley was gone. We looked everywhere, but it was like she just disappeared and . . . I'm sorry."

"It's okay," I said. "She's safe. We're all safe."

Kayla went to Ainsley and held her hands. Their

familiar roles were reversed. Where Ainsley looked incredibly fragile, Kayla was confident and solid.

"Are you all right?" Kayla asked softly.

The look on Ainsley's face was priceless. Her mouth fell open in shock.

"You . . . you talked" was all she managed to say.

"You don't remember me talking to you inside?" Kayla asked.

Tears came to Ainsley's eyes and she shook her head. "I don't even remember *being* inside."

Theo shot me a questioning look. I shrugged as if to say, *Yeah, it's true.*

"Why?" Ainsley asked. "I mean, why are you talking now?"

Kayla gave her a tiny smile. "I guess I never felt as though I had anything worth saying, until you needed help."

"I wish I could remember," Ainsley said, crying.

"Maybe it's better you don't," Kayla said.

The two hugged. Hopefully they'd be able to rely on each other to make some sense out of what had happened. Or at least to help each other get over it.

Theo pulled me away from the two and spoke in a strained whisper. "They all think it was an earthquake. The kids, the parents, everybody."

"What are they saying about Ainsley being in the center of it?"

"Not a lot. I heard some rumblings about how they thought she was there to help clear the gym. You know, since she's always the one in charge. Nobody thinks she had anything to do with it."

"Good. That explanation makes a heck of a lot more sense than the truth."

"What is the truth, Marcus?" Theo asked. "Is this over?"

I looked around at the chaotic scene—the frightened kids, the destroyed gym—and at the brilliant canopy of stars shining down on it all from above.

"I sure hope so."

"Marcus!" Lu yelled.

She was on the back of Nate's ATV, standing up in the saddle behind Nate as he tore up to us and skidded to a stop. Lu leapt off the bike and threw her arms around me.

"I thought you were trapped down there!"

"We were," I said. "Ainsley got us to the tunnel back to the school. But she doesn't remember any of it."

"You're lucky, O'Mara," Nate said. "The whole deal collapsed. All those big boulders? Gone. They sank underground. Whatever was down there ain't anymore."

That clearing is now flat and empty like nothing was ever there."

Lu said, "We looked to see if the opening to the cavern was still there, but it's totally sealed off. What happened to the witches?"

"Buried. Along with their broken altar," I said. "I think whatever hold they had over Ainsley was snapped when the altar went down, just like in the other stories."

"Mr. Christmas!" came an angry voice.

It was the sour woman from the office. She strode up boldly, still wearing the Cat in the Hat hat, which looked even sillier given the circumstances.

"You have been suspended from this school and all of its functions. Do I need to call a police officer to escort you from—"

"Yes!" I exclaimed. "Call them over!"

"What!" Nate shouted in surprise. "What're you doing?"

"I want to make sure you get what you deserve," I said.

"Are you kiddin' me?" Nate exclaimed, furious. "I helped you!"

"I know," I said. "And I want to make sure you get the credit."

"Uh, you do?" he asked, totally confused.

"Absolutely!" I turned to the annoying lady and said,

"Nate's a hero. As soon as the earthquake hit, he risked his life to get kids out. Ainsley was in there trying to do the same thing, but she got trapped. If not for Nate, she might not have made it out alive."

"Is that true?" Ainsley said as she walked over to join us. "You saved me, Nate? I don't remember a thing."

Nate was thrown. "Uhhh, hey, don't listen to me. O'Mara knows what happened."

"If Nate hadn't been here, this disaster would have been far worse," I said. "He saved a whole lot of lives tonight."

I may have fudged some of the details. Okay, a lot of the details. But the bottom line was the absolute truth: Nate had saved a lot of people, including Ainsley and me.

Ainsley went right to Nate and gave him a big hug.

"Thank you," she said.

Nate was about as shocked as I'd ever seen anyone, ever. He wasn't sure how to react but then relaxed, gave in, and hugged her back.

"Hey, no problem," he said. "I'm just glad you're safe."

Theo and Lu did their best not to burst out laughing.

The cranky lady in the hat looked almost as confused as Nate did. Seeing Nate and Ainsley together must have been like a glimpse through the looking glass for her.

281

"Oh, I see," she said with disappointment. "That's very commendable, Mr. Christmas. Well done."

The woman backed off awkwardly and left. Her thunder was completely gone. She really wanted to bust Nate for something.

Nate got off his bike, took Lu and me by the arms, and led us away from the others.

"You gonna tell me exactly what happened?" he asked.

"What happened is you're a hero," I said. "Yeah, I made up some stuff, but what you really did was way bigger than that. You saved a lot of lives."

Nate looked baffled. He was wrestling with pride, fear, joy, and total confusion.

"So what were those people? I mean, they weren't human."

"Sometimes things happen that can't be explained," I said. "This is one of those times. But it's over. Martin and Tomac won't be coming back to school. And I don't think there are going to be any more weird accidents either. You did a good thing tonight, Nate. Better you just let it go and don't try to understand."

Nate looked sick. He backed away toward his bike.

"Yeah, maybe you're right," he said. "I'm getting outta here before anything else happens."

"Good idea," I said.

"Just one more thing," he said.

"What's that?"

"I don't know who you guys are, but I'll ride with you anytime."

"I'll remember that," I said.

He was about to get on his bike when he thought of something else. He walked over to Kayla, who was standing with Theo. As he approached, Kayla moved a little closer to Theo for protection. Theo puffed up his chest and stood tall to protect her.

"Easy, Poindexter," Nate said to Theo dismissively. "Don't get all twitchy."

Theo backed off, relieved that he didn't have to protect Kayla from the bully.

Nate turned to Kayla.

"Look, uh, Kayla," he said awkwardly, "I've been kind of a jerk to you. I'm sorry. It won't happen again."

Kayla smiled sweetly and said, "Thanks."

Nate perked up with surprise. "Hey, you talked! Did everybody hear that? I got her to talk! I did it! I win the bet! Yeah!"

We all reacted with blank stares. Nate got the message and calmed down.

"Uh, oh, never mind," he said, embarrassed. "I get it. Not cool. Sorry."

He skulked off toward his bike, but Ainsley got in his

way. Nate froze. The two stood staring at one another. Everybody was ready for Ainsley to tee off on him. Including Nate.

Ainsley smiled and said, "Could you give me a ride home? I'm really tired."

Nate brightened.

"Uh, yeah, sure. Hop on!"

"Wait one second," she said to him, and then came over to me and Lu.

"You okay?" I asked.

"I have no idea," she said. "I'm not exactly sure why, but I feel like I should thank you guys."

"No worries," Lu said. "We're just happy everybody's okay."

"There's more to this than you're saying, isn't there?" Ainsley asked.

"Maybe," I said with a chuckle. "But it's over now. The story's finished."

Ainsley gave me a confused look, then nodded thoughtfully. I wondered if she would ever have any memories of her brief reign as high priestess of the Black Moon Circle. I sure hope not.

She backed toward Nate's bike and said, "See you guys on Monday? Big cleanup to do here. Everybody's gotta pitch in!"

She was back to her old self. That didn't take long.

"Yeah, good luck with that," I said.

"Bye, Ainsley," Lu added.

Ainsley gave us a quick wave and hopped on the back of Nate's bike. Nate fired up the engine, gave me a big smile and a thumbs-up. With a roar, the two took off and rode into the night.

"I guess stranger things than that have happened," Theo said as he walked up with Kayla.

"Gee, you think?" Lu said.

"Ainsley has no memory of what she almost did," Kayla said.

"Hopefully she never will," I added. "She was being controlled by some very bad people. But they won't bother her anymore."

"I'm not so sure I want to know who they were," Kayla said.

"You don't," Theo said with authority. "It's best you try to forget the whole thing. I know I'm going to."

"You saved her, Kayla," Lu said. "You saved everyone."

"I was just trying to help her," she said. "Ainsley's always been so nice to me."

"Things are going to get a lot better around here," I said. "For everybody."

"Kayla!" someone shouted.

A guy stood on the edge of the parking lot waving to her. He looked pretty worried. No big surprise.

"My dad," Kayla said. "See you guys on Monday?"

We all exchanged glances, not knowing what to say.

"No," Theo finally said, taking the bullet. "We came here to try and put things right. Now we've got to go home."

We all looked to Kayla, wondering how she would react to that. She thought about it and nodded as if she understood. Or maybe she didn't really want to understand, but she accepted it.

"I knew you guys were a little different," she said. "Different is good."

"I always thought so," Lu said with a smile.

After a few quick hugs, with Theo getting the longest along with a quick kiss on the cheek, Kayla ran off to her father. She looked every bit like a princess running home from the ball.

A very strange and exciting ball.

I reached around my neck and pulled out the Paradox key.

"Ready to go home?" I said.

"Absolutely," Theo replied.

"Can't wait," Lu added.

The three of us walked past random kids and emergency personnel, headed for the school and the first door we could find.

"Hey," Lu said, "it's Halloween. What are *we* going to go as?"

"A hibernating bear," Theo replied without hesitation. "I need a nap."

"What about you, Marcus?" Lu asked.

"I'm done with Halloween. As far as I'm concerned, from now on it's a straight shot from summer to Thanksgiving. No stops in between."

I inserted the Paradox key into a door that wasn't visible from the parking lot and opened it to reveal the Library. Holding the door open, I let Lu and Theo enter first. Before going in myself, I took one last look at Coppell Middle School, then lifted my gaze to the sky, where the stars seemed a little less bright.

"Hey," I asked as I followed them through, "when's the next black moon on Halloween?"

CHAPTER
19

"So is the Black Moon Circle done for good this time?" Lu asked. "Or will they just hang around until they find another victim, and try it again?"

Everett sat at the circulation desk reading through the red book that now held the rest of the story.

"I do believe this time they are finished," he replied.

"What makes you think this time is any different from the others?" Theo asked while tugging thoughtfully on his ear.

"In all the other accounts of their shenanigans there was no mention of the agents from the Library destroying any of their totems or talismans. You not only demolished the altar, you also ruined the very powerful items they used to conjure their magic."

"Yeah, and let's not forget the whole 'burying the entire coven under tons of rocks' thing," Lu added.

"Aye," Everett said. "I'll never say never to anything, but I'd be surprised if another story turned up about them. I'm thinking you put that coven out of business for good, which means there's only one thing left to do."

"What's that?" Theo asked.

"A finished book needs a title," Everett said with a wink.

All eyes went to me. I had actually given this a little thought.

"This was Ainsley's story," I said. "But there were a lot of players. Not all of them were good. Without them, Ainsley would never have been in danger. It was their hatred and anger that made it all happen. That's what the story was really about."

"So what do you want to call it?" Theo asked.

"Black Moon Rising."

Theo and Lu smiled with delight.

"Yeah!" Lu exclaimed. "I'd read that book."

"Read, yes," Theo said. "I'd just as soon not have to live through it again."

"Black Moon Rising it is," Everett announced. "Now, one more piece of business."

He slid the book over to me.

"Time for you to return the book," he said as he

opened the cover to the page where I had signed my name.

"What do I do?" I asked.

"Cross your name out, lad," he said.

He handed me the same old-fashioned pen I had used to sign my name. Checking out the book was another little piece of Library magic that allowed us to become part of the story. Now the story was over. The book was finished. I took the pen and with one quick swipe put a dark line through my name.

"That's it?" I asked.

Everett took the book from me and closed it.

"Aye. Now I find a spot for it with the other finished books. I believe I'll be shelving it under *Witchcraft*."

"And that means it's time to get back to real life," I said.

Theo, Lu, and I stood, ready to hit the exit.

"Real life," Theo repeated, then looked to Lu. "Did you tell your parents about that C in science yet?"

Lu shrugged. "No, but I'm not sweating it anymore. It's crazy to stress about not being perfect all the time."

"Yeah," I said. "Perfect isn't good. You might have witches coming after you to try and make you their high priestess."

"Exactly!" Lu said with a chuckle. "My parents'll just have to accept that I'm always trying my best."

"What about you, Marcus?" Everett asked. "Given any thought to what you might do for an extracurricular activity?"

"You mean being an agent for the Library isn't enough?" Theo asked.

"It would be, if my parents knew," I said. "So I'm going to tell them."

The three of them stood up straight as if they'd been shocked by a jolt of electricity.

"Seriously?" Theo exclaimed. "You're going to tell them?"

"Bad idea, Marcus," Lu said. "If you tell them they'll tell my parents and they'll tell Theo's and then none of us will be allowed to come back."

"Have you thought this through?" Everett asked, frowning.

"Absolutely," I replied. "I'm going to tell my parents they're absolutely right. I need to have other interests that'll help me grow and meet new people, so I decided to volunteer at the library. The school library. They're always looking for extra help."

They all stared at me with their mouths open, as if they didn't quite understand what I was saying.

"The school library?" Lu said, dumbfounded. "You mean like . . . at school?"

"Yeah. You didn't think I was going to tell them about *this* place, did you? Are you crazy?"

There were relieved breaths let out all around.

"I figure it's a good cover in case anybody hears us talking about the Library. Hopefully it'll get my parents off my back until track season in the spring."

Lu gave me a playful shove. "Dork."

The three of us started for the door that would bring us back to my bedroom.

"Oh," Everett called out, "almost forgot."

We turned back to him as he tossed a jet-black book onto the circulation desk.

"I believe I found it," he declared.

"Found what?" I asked.

"The stories you've been looking for. Turns out there aren't two stories, only one."

"What are you talking about?" Lu asked, confused.

"It's a story about a young woman who's gone missing," he said.

Lu went rigid. "My cousin? That's her story? Are you sure?"

"Jenny Feng's her name?"

"Yes!" Lu exclaimed. "You found her?"

"I found her story," Everett replied. "I'm afraid your fears are justified. She's in the middle of a disruption."

Lu grabbed for the book eagerly.

"Does it say what happened to her?" she asked.

"Up to a point. But she's still missing. That story doesn't say why; it only sets the stage."

"What do you mean, there's only one story?" Theo asked suspiciously.

"It seems Jenny's story began when she had her fortune told by a machine at an amusement park."

The news hit Theo with such force he had to sit back down.

"The machine at Playland?" he asked, his voice barely above a whisper. "The one that told my fortune?"

"Aye," Everett said. "It looks as though something is definitely amiss there."

"'Life as you know it will end on your fourteenth birthday,'" Theo muttered numbly. He had every word of his fortune memorized. "So I really am in trouble. I'm not sure if I'm glad you found the book, or really, really scared."

I took the black book from Lu and flipped through a few pages. There was a story there. A new story.

Only this one was about my friends.